ORC EROICA

CONJECTURE CHRONICLES

Characters

Bash

An Orc Hero respected by all members of his race. He is a mighty warrior who has laid waste to his enemies on multiple battlefields.

> "The objective of my journey is a private matter. In short, I am in pursuit of something."

Zell

Bash's old war buddy, a curious and lively fairy. After a chance meeting on the road, the two rekindle their partnership when Zell decides to join Bash on his journey.

> "So you've set out on a journey to find a bride, right, Boss?"

Judith

A rookie knight from the Fortified City of Krassel. She holds a strong grudge against all orcs after a tragic incident in her past...

"I refuse to let an *orc* waste my precious time!"

Thunder Sonia

An Elf Archmage and one of the great heroes who defeated the Demon Lord during the war. Her fate seems to be deeply intertwined with Bash's...

"People who really have a calling in life don't just sit around. They're already out there, taking action."

As their heavy paws hit the ground, there was a dull flash. Three of the bugbears were turned instantly into mincemeat.

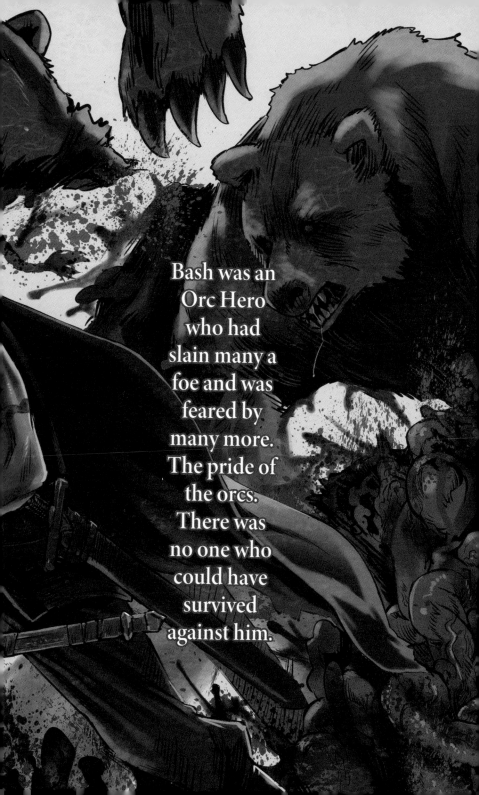

Bash was an Orc Hero who had slain many a foe and was feared by many more. The pride of the orcs. There was no one who could have survived against him.

ORC EROICA

CONTENTS

Orc Eroica

CONJECTURE CHRONICLES

1

Rifujin na Magonote

Illustration by
Asanagi

YEN ON
New York

ORC EROICA 1

Rifujin na Magonote

Translation by Evie Lund
Cover art by Asanagi

ORC EIYU MONOGATARI Volume 1 SONTAKU RETSUDEN
©Rifujin na Magonote, Asanagi 2020
First Published in Japan in 2020 by KADOKAWA CORPORATION, Tokyo.
English translation rights arranged with KADOKAWA CORPORATION, Tokyo through
TUTTLE-MORI AGENCY, INC., Tokyo.

Yen On
150 West 30th Street, 19th Floor
New York, NY 10001

Visit us at yenpress.com
facebook.com/yenpress
twitter.com/yenpress
yenpress.tumblr.com
instagram.com/yenpress

First Yen On Edition: November 2021

Yen On is an imprint of Yen Press, LLC.
The Yen On name and logo are trademarks of Yen Press, LLC.

Library of Congress Cataloging-in-Publication Data
Names: Na Magonote, Rifujin, author. | Asanagi, illustrator. | Lund, Evie, translator.
Title: Orc eroica / Rifujin na Magonote ; illustration by Asanagi ; translated by Evie Lund.
Other titles: Orc eiyuu monogatari. English
Description: First Yen On edition. | New York, NY : Yen On, 2021–
Identifiers: LCCN 2021038197 | ISBN 9781975334338 (v. 1 ; trade paperback)
Subjects: LCGFT: Fantasy fiction. | Light novels.
Classification: LCC PL873.5.A17 O7313 2021 | DDC 895.63/6—dc23
LC record available at https://lccn.loc.gov/2021038197

ISBNs: 978-1-9753-3433-8 (paperback)
        978-1-9753-3434-5 (ebook)

10 9 8 7 6 5 4 3 2 1

LSC-C

Printed in the United States of America

忖度 (*sontaku*) "conjecture, surmise"; to make an assumption or guess about the feelings of another, and to then demonstrate care or consideration for the other party based on this.

(Source: Wikipedia Japan)

PROLOGUE

Long ago, there raged a great and terrible war.

A grueling, interminable, and truly bloody conflict.

The entire continent of Vastonia became a battleground, swallowed up by the seemingly endless mires of combat.

None could recall what had originally sparked the fighting.

According to elven legend, the cause of it all had been when the prince of demons had kidnapped the princess of the kingdom of humans. The dwarves, however, told a different tale. They said it all began when the human king had the village of the demons ransacked and destroyed.

Putting the various legends together, it was easy enough to guess that the conflict began between humans and demons. But today, there were none still alive to tell the tale of who struck the first blow.

History tells us that the war lasted for more than five thousand years.

The continent of Vastonia was home to no less than twelve distinct races, and all were swept up in the conflict.

All believed the fighting would last forever. Children were born in war. Their parents were born in war. Their grandparents were born in war. And so on. It was the same for everyone. There were no memories of peacetime. Even the elves, who could live for five hundred years, were no different in this respect.

All grew up believing their destiny lay in becoming soldiers. And all believed their children and grandchildren would be born to a similar fate, to battle on forevermore. They were all stuck fighting a war that they could see no way to bring to an end, for causes none could recall, and for reasons no one even thought to question.

But then one day, without warning, the war ended.

No one could recall how it began, but all would remember what brought the great war to its conclusion.

It was the Demon Lord Geddigs.

When he appeared, the tides of war suddenly shifted.

He was a truly remarkable figure.

He was overflowing with charisma, certainly far more than any other Demon Lord in ages past. In his hundred-year reign as ruler, he established an alliance spearheaded by the demons, which banded them together with six other races: the ogres, the fairies, the harpies, the succubi, the lizardmen, and the orcs. Known as the Coalition of Seven, it was the first time these races had worked together, and with a new sense of battle doctrine alive within them, they managed to dominate the remaining four human-led tribes, expanding their sphere of influence over a wider terrain than ever before.

It was a terrible tragedy for the human-led faction, known as the Alliance of Four Races.

Never before had those seven other races formed a united front against them.

The harpies would speedily airlift the ogres, who were innately slow due to their hulking size. The succubi would spread their peach-hued, fog-like charm mist across the marshlands, and then the lizardmen, who were immune to this magical effect, would charge across the marsh to press the attack. Such coordination had never occurred before among those races, except by happenstance. The Alliance of Four, which had long been cooperating, was utterly powerless to resist.

But at the same time, an opportunity presented itself.

The army brought together by the Demon Lord Geddigs and formed of seven united races was like an impenetrable slab of stone. Yet despite the vast strength and sparkling charisma he possessed, Geddigs himself represented a huge weak point.

This vulnerability possessed by Geddigs the demon—rather than Geddigs the king—was unknown to the Alliance of Four, of course.

But they could more easily predict what fate would await them—their complete and total annihilation—unless, of course, the figurehead Geddigs could be toppled.

And so the Demon Lord became their target.

During the battle of Remium Plateau, a suicide squad led by four main players infiltrated deep into the demon army and attacked Geddigs. The four leaders consisted of the Human Prince Nazar, the Elf Archmage Thunder Sonia, the Dwarf Battlelord Dradoradobanga, and the Beastkin Champion Rett.

There were many casualties. Battlelord Dradoradobanga and Beastkin Champion Rett lost their lives in the final fight against Geddigs, and over half of the suicide squad did not survive.

Though Geddigs was slain, Human Prince Nazar also incurred heavy injuries during the battle and was forced to withdraw.

There was a dramatic change following the death of Geddigs.

With his loss, the Coalition of Seven had lost their leader. With astonishing rapidity, their union began to fall apart.

There was no one in place to succeed Geddigs.

Without anyone in charge to even issue the most basic of orders, the coalition's chain of command collapsed in the face of heavy attacks.

And with the seven races scrambling, waiting for orders that would never come, the four races of the human faction easily moved in and mopped up.

If the leaders of each race hadn't finally stepped in and begun to take charge of their own factions, several of the races may have gone completely extinct during the ensuing conflict.

The Coalition of Seven disbanded, rejecting demon law and returning to fighting as separate, hostile armies, as they had done before Geddigs had united them all.

For tactical reasons, the seven had primarily paired off—ogres with harpies, succubi with lizardmen, and orcs with fairies. But without leadership, these mini-factions could no longer operate effectively in tandem and were cut down at every turn.

Five years passed after the death of Geddigs. And in those five years, the seven races had lost control of all their territory.

Every piece of land they had obtained over the past hundred years, lost.

The Coalition of Seven expected to be completely overthrown, their demise a foregone conclusion.

Such was the power of the remaining four races.

But then peace talks were suggested. Human Prince Nazar was the one to bring up this option during a meeting of the Alliance of Four. *"Why not give them a second chance?"* he asked. *"Why not offer peace?"*

The people also echoed this sentiment. It had been a long war. The last hundred years in particular had been especially brutal and bloody. They were all tired of fighting.

The truth of it was that the Alliance of Four was long past its limits.

In the past hundred years of Geddigs's rule, the four races had all suffered heavy reductions in population. The humans, elves, dwarves, and beastkin were dwindling in number.

Life expectancy rates had taken a nosedive, and there was no longer any faith that they would be able to raise the next generation of children to adulthood.

Everyone wanted to rest. They'd all had enough.

What would happen if the seven races somehow struggled free of the corner they were trapped in, banded together once more, and launched another attack? Could the human faction win a second time?

What would happen next? Perhaps this war would only lead to mutually assured destruction if it was allowed to continue.

In this brief pocket of opportunity, where the human faction had the right to speak, their message had to be one of peace.

So said Nazar.

The higher-ups of the three other races of the human faction were said to have their doubts. "*They'll never abide by the rules of peace,*" they remarked darkly. But when peace talks were actually offered, a strange thing happened. The other races all fell in line.

Even the ogres, whose ability to process language was always in doubt, and the orcs, who relished nothing more in life than the opportunity to fight, pillage, and steal enemy women, accepted the conditions that put them at a disadvantage and agreed to peace.

And so the war ended.

At long last, the conflict was over.

◆

Three years passed.

Our tale now brings us to the third year of what has been dubbed the Age of Peace.

After a brief period during which everyone was stunned to find that the long war was truly over, they began to rebuild. The towns that had been ravaged by war began to return to life. Merchants began to trade with the different races, babies were born, and there were signs that the population was beginning to increase again. Gradually, all began to open their eyes to peace and to embark upon new challenges.

Education, the arts, trade, entertainment...all the things that had been cast aside and disregarded during wartime were suddenly exalted, and the societies of the different races began to undergo rapid change.

The Age of Peace had passed through its first act, and now the stage was set for what would come next.

Our story begins during this moment in time, in a country that is home to one of the defeated races of war:

The country of the orcs.

ORC

Book One

The Fortified City of Krassel Saga

EROICA

1

A Hero Goes Forth

Orcs.

Green skin, long tusks, and sturdy, chiseled bodies resistant to poison and disease. A race built for war.

It is also worth mentioning that they possess a voracious carnal appetite.

For the orcs, breeding isn't just a means to propagate the species. It's just as much for everyday relaxation and recreation.

Fight, feast, fuck. Repeat.

The orcs count success in battle equally by the number of heads they take and by the number of children they sire after the fighting.

Die in glory on the battlefield and leave plenty of offspring behind. That is the legacy every orc aspires toward.

They have robust bodies and high levels of fertility.

What more could any race need? But the truth is that there is one area in which the orc race is sorely lacking...

...There are no female orcs, only males. In order to reproduce, they need access to the wombs of women belonging to other races.

They captured female soldiers during wartime and used them as broodmares to birth child after child until their bodies gave out and they could birth no more. This is a major reason why the other races hated the orcs with the fire of a thousand suns.

"Hey, look over there. Isn't that the so-called Hero?"

Bash.

The one by that name was an orc to surpass all others, a formidable warrior.

He was swifter to leap into battle than any other and remained on the front line longer than anyone else. And naturally, he defeated many, many more enemies than any other as well.

Many orcs owed their lives to him, and many a battle had been led to victory by the heroic actions of Bash.

Brave enough to face off against even the strongest of enemies, the sight of Bash in battle would make any spectator think to themselves, *Surely, this is the pinnacle of the orc race.*

And for all these courageous deeds, he had been given the title of Hero.

Hero. One who was revered for their bravery.

To an orc, there could be no greater title, no greater validation of one's strength.

All orcs admired Bash very much indeed.

"The Hero! Aw man, he's so cool!"

"Ya know, I'd love ta hear the story of how he defeated the Black Head that one time..."

Along with the title of Hero, Bash had everything an orc could want—

A big house. The finest weaponry. More food than he could possibly eat. More special privileges than he could possibly ever cash in. And the respect and admiration of every orc alive.

He had everything...everything all young orcs dreamed of.

"Ah...I apologize, but I was actually just about to leave..."

"Idiots! Can't you see he's just trying to have a quiet drink in peace?!"

"Oh, yikes, our bad... Sorry, I forgot we don't have the right ta approach a Hero in public an' make demands on his time!"

But Bash had a big problem, a problem that weighed on his mind continually.

Yes, from the outside, he appeared to have everything he could want, but in truth, there was one thing he'd never been able to get.

Ah, perhaps that was phrased incorrectly. It wasn't so much about him wanting to *get* something as wanting to *lose* something, if you can read between the lines...

Something he wanted to dispose of forever, like an ancient ring cast into the flames of an undying fire...

"No, man, come on! I wanna hear the Hero speak! I wanna know what kinda women he likes!"

"What kinda women he likes? It's gotta be human women, right?"

"Are ya outta yer mind?! He's a freakin' Hero, y'know? During the battles, he musta bedded so many humans an' elves. I bet he's sick o' the ladies! I ain't seen him around the Breeding Grounds lately, have you?!"

"Sick of humans an' elves? Wait, ya can't be suggestin' it's dragonewts he's into, can ya?! That legendary race?!"

"Anythin's possible! He's a Hero, after all!"

This evening, Bash was sitting by himself at the tavern's bar, nursing a fire whiskey and agonizing over his particular problem once again.

How, though? How to lose it?

The act itself was easily done. But in the land of the orcs, Bash stuck out like a sore thumb, so famous was he. Someone was bound to find out. And if the truth was revealed, he would lose everything. That was for certain.

As a Hero among orcs—hell, forget the Hero part—as a virile, manly orc, the shame of people knowing his big secret would crush him.

The second word got out, Bash's pride and dignity would be in tatters.

The respect given to him by all orckind would instantly turn into scorn and ridicule.

Bash's already meager self-esteem would be obliterated, and he'd have to go through life wearing a sack over his head...if he could even bear to go on with life at all.

"I'm gonna ask him!"

"Don't! It's disrespectful."

"I just wanna ask him about his best lay! That ain't so disrespectful a question, is it? Was it a human warrior? An elf tavern owner? A rich beastkin's only daughter? I gotta know!"

Bash got to his feet.

He was an even six foot five. A bit short for an orc, but his body bore many scars, which told the stories of the countless battles he'd fought. His taut muscles were double the size of any other orc's in the bar.

He was also extremely stoic in terms of his personality, radiating an aura of dignity and unapproachability at all times.

He turned and faced the drunk young orc, who still seemed determined to engage him in bawdy conversation. Bash was scowling.

"..."

The approaching orc froze.

"S-sorry, sir! This guy, he don't know when to shut up! Gets a little rowdy on the sauce, ya know...?"

The orc's companion bowed frantically before Bash.

As a rule, orcs never lowered their heads, and certainly not in response to a mere scowl.

But Bash was a Hero. Failing to bow before such an orc would be a grave offense.

"Hmph." Bash snorted once. Then he stomped across the tavern, heading for the door.

"Aw man, he really is cool..."

All the orcs seated nearby let out sighs and murmurs of admiration.

Bash's strength and charisma...it was overwhelming.

Any other orc but Bash would have welcomed the admiring stares of his younger fellows and grinned as he boasted of his many deeds.

What's that, squirt? Ya wanna hear my tales of greatness? Ga-ha-ha! Very well then, I'll tell ya. It was durin' the battle of Arkansel Plains. I was facin' off against a herd of enemy fighters, when one of 'em comes up an' says ta me...

Well, there's nothing wrong with that.

In orc society, it was considered only warrior-like to brag about one's prowess on the battlefield. What's wrong with tooting one's own horn after a battle well fought? It was a completely acceptable practice.

And if the superior orc was in a bad mood that day, maybe he'd beat up on the younger orcs. Just a little.

Shut yer traps, ya filthy maggots! Can't ya see an orc's just tryin' ta have a quiet drink in peace?!

That would be fine, too. Beating the younger generation into shape was another way for an orc to show off his superiority.

Yes, being punched in the jaw by an orc of Bash's caliber would be like a dream come true to these young orcs. What a memory to treasure. What a tale to tell!

But what Bash did was even cooler.

His actions spoke volumes. They gave the impression: *Impudent little orcs like you don't even register on my radar.*

Yes, a truly strong orc would respond in this way.

That was how you identified a real warrior. A true Hero like Bash didn't have the time to pay attention to every wide-eyed, drunken young orc who worshipped him in a tavern.

Just being able to drink the same booze as Bash, in the same tavern as Bash.

That was more than honor enough for the younglings. In the flesh, Bash was so cool that simply being in his presence was greater than any thrill they'd had in life thus far.

Enough to make their chests swell with emotion.

"Aw man! I'd give anythin' ta be like him!"

"You fool! You'll never be like him! No one's like him!"

"All right, all right! I just wanted ta hear it from the orc himself... I wanted ta know how many women he's had!"

Bash sighed, the voices of the young orcs carrying through the door of the tavern.

What would they think if they could see Bash scurrying home, his broad back stooped, looking small and weak? Taking tiny shuffling steps, as if deeply afraid of something unseen?

The young orcs had gotten to Bash, their words hitting him right in the sore spot.

How many women he'd had?

Which one was best in the sack?

How could he have possibly answered such questions?

Bash's biggest insecurity, his biggest complex... For this admirable orc who had it all, there was one thing he was desperate to be rid of.

And that thing was...

"Ah, how I envy him! Man, it blows my mind just tryin' ta guess how many women he's stuck it to!"

...*Zero. It's zero.*

Bash was a virgin.

Bash was born during the long war.

In the midst of the conflict, a human woman was captured, taken prisoner, and subjected to repeated violation. A green orc pup slithered from her womb as she breathed her last.

That orc was Bash.

At the age of five, Bash first held a sword. At ten, he joined his first battle and felled his first foe.

Even among war-loving orcs, ten was very young to have one's first taste of battle.

Indeed, ten years old was a ridiculous age to join full-grown orcs in all-out war.

But at that time, even a ten-year-old orc was likely to return from battle alive; such was the success of the battle doctrines put in place by the Demon Lord Geddigs.

Or at least, they were *likely* to return alive.

Fortunately, Bash did survive.

In that first year of fighting, Bash came close to death many times. But by the second year, he had become an accomplished warrior, and by the third year, he had become one of the best. In his fourth year, he really did become the best. His fifth year saw him become famous among all orckind as one of the strongest orcs who had ever lived.

A formidable, legendary warrior.

Indeed, Bash was a prodigy when it came to battle.

The battlefield was harsh, but wherever Bash went, things were different.

Bash's position on the battlefield was marked by a rain of human, elf, and dwarf blood. Guts and entrails were strewn all over the ground in his general radius.

Bash would take on and annihilate any foe who came his way.

The strongest brawler, the nimblest swordsman, the so-called demigods of battle—all fell to Bash's attacks as he racked up kill after kill.

And Bash never rested.

After each victory, it was on to the next encounter.

Battle after battle, with barely a pause in between.

This mighty warrior didn't even know what it meant to be tired. He battled on, day and night.

He paused only once every three days, sprinkling medicinal fairy dust over himself to force sleep for just a little while.

Bash never thought to question any of this. He was just doing what he was expected to do as an orc warrior.

But Bash's battle prowess was immense.

Citizens of each country began to speak in fearful whispers of the "super orc."

Those who had witnessed Bash at work in battle and escaped to tell the tale claimed he was: "*The very incarnation of the god of war, Gudagoza himself.*"

When the war was over, the human commander-in-chief himself was heard saying: "*If that orc had shown up on the battlefield five years earlier, then I daresay we are the ones who would have ended up tasting defeat.*"

Fundamentally, though, Bash was an incredibly private and modest person.

He saw himself as just another soldier, albeit one who happened to possess incredible strength.

Despite his ability to dominate in battle, he felt powerless to change his overall situation.

The Demon Lord Geddigs was toppled in Bash's tenth year of fighting, and five years later, the war was brought to an end.

While Bash's side had lost, Bash himself attained the title of Hero, and many other things besides.

A grand house, more food than he could eat, the finest weaponry, and the respectful gaze of every orc in the land.

But with all this came a realization.

A truly harsh realization.

The realization that even orcs had more to live for than the battlefield.

Once the fighting was done, the generally agreed-upon practice was to drag a woman home by the hair and have one's way with her.

By the time the war was over for good, not a single one of the warriors Bash had fought alongside remained a virgin.

Bash felt it was far too late to admit the truth.

The truth that he had zero carnal experience. That he was a virgin, and all the rest.

The realization came quite late for Bash. If only the war was still ongoing, things might have been different.

If the war raged on, Bash could have decimated the enemy forces, selected a surviving warrior, dragged her back to base, and gloriously unburdened himself from the stigma of his virginity. Then, after practicing on enough women, he could bring home the one he liked best and have her pop out a baby orc or two. That was what he should have done.

But now it was too late.

The Coalition of Seven, to which the orcs belonged, had lost.

The orcs, too, had opted for peace.

They had signed a treaty, agreeing to their unconditional surrender.

And one of the conditions of the treaty had been that orcs would no longer *engage in nonconsensual coitus with members of different races.*

In other words, no sex without the lady's express consent.

It sounds reasonable enough, right? But to orcs, such a concept was absurd.

If forced mating was outlawed, how was the orc race to reproduce? They would surely die out.

But they had no other choice than to accept.

Better hypothetical extinction than imminent extinction.

Many would have preferred death. There were calls to keep on fighting down to the last orc. But the Orc King overruled his people.

Then, in a stroke of good fortune, the other races opted to send their convicted criminals over to the orcs as a peace offering, quelling the orcs' fears of eventual extinction due to a lack of breeding partners. Enough women were sent, with enough fertile years among them, to birth just the amount of young needed to keep the orc population going.

So, to be honest, Bash could have flung his virginity to the winds long ago.

All he had to do was stroll on down to the Breeding Grounds and make use of that peace offering the other races had sent. Simple.

At the Breeding Grounds, mating priority was given based on an orc's past deeds in battle. Bash wouldn't even have had to wait in line. His virginity could have been done away with in the blink of an eye.

But if Bash went to the Breeding Grounds, there would be other orcs there just wandering about.

How excited they would be to catch a glimpse of a decorated war hero in the act of mating.

Now, this might go without saying, but a virgin could hardly be expected to put on a showstopping sexual performance.

Bash knew his first time would involve huge amounts of fumbling, bumbling, and embarrassment—a shameful display of sweaty indignity.

Yes, in the land of the orcs, to dispose of one's virginity was to make evident the existence of one's virginity itself.

There was no way Bash could have avoided this fate.

And there was no way he would subject himself to such abject humiliation.

The prospect alone would make any man shrink, but Bash was an orc, and a Hero at that.

Bash stood alone, an exalted and famed figure among orcs. If people found out that this Hero was actually a virgin, the pride of the entire orc race would be wounded.

And so Bash needed to hide the truth of his virginity for the rest of his life.

That isn't to say that Bash had resigned himself to a life of abstinence.

No, he was a young, virile orc.

His drive to throw down a woman and put a child in her belly was as strong as any other's.

And it wasn't just his natural, carnal urges we had to consider.

Every strong warrior had the duty to pass down their genes to their offspring.

Additionally, the Orc King was always imploring the people to go down to the Breeding Grounds and impregnate as many of the women as possible.

Ah, but to have one's virginity discovered...the humiliation.

There was no greater shame known among orckind.

Bash may have been a virgin, but he still had his pride as a Hero.

And he would have hated to see disappointment replace the look of admiration in the eyes of the young orcs who gazed fawningly at him in taverns.

And so Bash felt he was stuck in a hopeless situation. He thought about it all the time.

For three entire years, since the war ended, he thought of little else.

To make matters worse, he was twenty-eight years old.

He had just turned twenty-eight that year.

In two more years, he would be a thirty-year-old virgin. Well, looking on the bright side, at least he'd turn into a wizard.

That's not a joke, by the way. An orc who reached thirty years old without engaging in carnal activity really would acquire magical powers, even without any sort of training.

In fact, orc mages were extremely gifted warriors in battle.

Orcs were already formidable foes. Now imagine them with magic.

Orc mages were raised in isolated communities free from the temptation of women. Once their magical powers activated, a crest appeared on their foreheads.

The orcs bearing such a crest were treated with reverence. Well, to a point.

The crest was proof that they had exercised self-control for thirty long years, all for the sake of their nation.

But those were orc mages. For an ordinary orc warrior to manifest such a crest... the embarrassment was too much to comprehend.

Besides, the people had long had a saying... *"Orc mages are the shame of all orcs."*

Orcs didn't consider female warrior opponents *defeated* until they'd had their way with them. So orc mages, who battled for many years without ever performing this finishing act, were seen as weaklings with zero confirmed *conquests*.

They were shameful specimens of orcs.

Bash would rather have expired on the battlefield in a puddle of his own blood than suffer that fate.

And he only had two years left to go.

His virginity would expose itself all on its own, even if he never breathed a word.

"No...I'm gonna do it."

Right then and right there, Bash made up his mind once and for all.

That morning, Bash awoke and picked up his trusty greatsword.

His blade was meticulously maintained. On his sixth year of battle, he had rescued an entire unit of the demon army, and the sword had been gifted to him by the general to honor this deed.

It was imbued with magic. Thick and strong, it would never rust or lose any of its sharpness.

The robust nature of the sword meant that Bash could lose himself in battle, never having to worry about broken weaponry.

The sword was almost like a companion to Bash.

He slung it across his back and pulled on his armor. As an orc rose through the ranks, he won the right to don increasingly bulky armor.

As a Hero, Bash was free to wear full-body armor if he so wished, but instead, he continued to wear the light armor he had grown accustomed to.

Besides, after a full day of fighting, even the strongest of armor would end up shattered. *No point in wearing it at all, really,* thought Bash, giving his house a basic sweep and clean.

Orcs were surprisingly neat and skilled at keeping things clean and tidy. On the battlefield, they often needed to conceal their tracks as they closed in on the enemy. *"Only a fool leaves behind footprints,"* they believed.

Bash was especially good at cleaning.

Today, though, only a light clean was needed.

After putting things in their proper places, Bash left the house.

"..."

Upon exiting, Bash turned back for one last look.

Bash's house was the second-largest in the orc homeland. It was far too big for a single orc like him.

You might think he was so famous to have a full house at all times and host raucous, drunken parties where he regaled his guests with his tales of battlefield glory.

But Bash was reclusive and introverted, and trying desperately to keep his virginity a secret, so he permitted no guests.

Telling tales of glory would mean he would have to talk about his experiences with women.

Bash turned on his heel and set out along the path toward his destination.

"Oh, it's *Bash!*"

As he walked down the road, a few orc soldiers stood respectfully aside to let him pass, all of them blushing.

Usually, when two orcs met on the road, one would be sure to bellow: *Ya wanna pass?! Ya gotta kill me first! But be quick, before I rip yer head right off yer neck!*

Yes, that would be the usual greeting for orc soldiers like these.

"Aw man! The Hero looks cooler than ever!"

"He's headin' in the direction of the elder's house! What's he gonna discuss with him, I wonder?!"

"Maybe it's about becomin' the next elder?!"

"What?! Bash becomin' the next elder?! That would be freakin' amazin'! Man, I'd be first in line ta swear fealty to him!"

"You? First in line? Pah! You'd be eatin' my dust!"

As the voices of the soldier orcs carried on the breeze behind him, Bash arrived at his destination: a large house.

It was constructed of giant bones and colossal tree trunks. The largest and grandest house in the orc village.

Bash walked into the great hall, where several fires were burning.

At the far end of the hall, a few orcs were seated on the floor, enjoying a meal together.

"Bash..."

"Father, Bash's here."

"Bash. Would you care to join us for a meal?"

The seated orcs all welcomed Bash warmly.

They were all orcs of Bash's generation, and yet every one of them admired him greatly.

Back when Bash was new to the battlefield, he had his haters. But now, every orc in the land wanted to be just like him.

After all, he was a hero to his people.

"So, Bash, you've come."

In the center of the group, one orc sat staring sharply at Bash.

He was seated right in the middle, the only one with a chair, which was extravagantly carved. He was a truly important orc.

He was approaching old age, with a white beard to prove it, but he was almost double the size of Bash. He had an iron hammer by his side that was almost as long as he was tall.

He was the Orc King, Nemesis.

He was a strong and savage warrior who had battled on the front lines right up until the very end of the war. A sort of father figure to all orcs, who all respected him as their king.

Bash also respected him and had sworn his fealty long ago.

"What did you wish to see me about?"

Nemesis's gaze was sharp and penetrating.

Any normal orc would foam at the mouth and swoon in a dead faint if subjected to such a look from Nemesis.

"..."

Bash, however, didn't flinch. He simply stared back at Nemesis, a determined fire glowing in his own eyes.

Nemesis laughed, impressed by Bash's determination.

"My sons. Leave us now."

Nemesis's sons rose from their meal to withdraw elsewhere.

Without a word of complaint, they simply picked up their food and left with it.

A private meeting between king and Hero. Despite their burning curiosity, they, too, were orcs who had fought through to the very end of the war.

An orc warrior always follows orders from above.

And so, despite their reluctance, they headed outside without complaint.

"..."

Once it was just the two of them, Bash sat down opposite Nemesis.

There was still food remaining, but neither reached for it.

"..."

"..."

For a moment, the two of them simply observed each other in silence.

The silence seemed endless. Especially for orcs, who love nothing more than to bellow at the tops of their voices whenever they get the chance.

But the silence couldn't last forever.

Just as the fire crackled and popped, Nemesis cleared his throat.

"Your eyes tell me that you have already set your heart on this choice."

"Yes, I—"

"There is no need to explain. I understand."

Nemesis shut Bash down, even as he was about to speak aloud his decision.

"I have heard, of course, that you are rarely ever seen around the Breeding Grounds."

Nemesis's sharp eyes narrowed, focusing on Bash.

"You are leaving to seek a wife."

"...!"

The orc society was a promiscuous one.

One woman would be shared among many males and bear many orc babies.

But in order to preserve an outstanding bloodline, decorated orc warriors were permitted special dispensation to take a wife.

A wife...in other words, a woman for the warrior's exclusive use.

Someone to take care of the general household and to provide children who belonged to that warrior alone.

To achieve such a prize... It wouldn't be an exaggeration to say this was the orcs' highest ideal of status and success.

A wife...was a special thing indeed.

Like a shiny medal granted to only a select few elite orcs.

Naturally, only the finest woman would do for such a trophy. A maiden with the rarest beauty, who had songs sung about her loveliness. Or a female warrior of such skill and prowess that she had overcome the limitations of her sex and risen to the highest rank in the army. Or a woman possessed of such extreme intellect that she was said to be a once-in-a-thousand-years genius.

Such a rare gem would the warrior orc pursue, woo, and take to wife. The more special and extraordinary the wife, the greater the orc warrior's reputation would be.

Bash was a legendary Hero among orcs, destined for the history books.

If he was to take a wife, it would have to be someone suitable.

No mere slave or ex-convict from the Breeding Grounds would do for such an exalted man as he.

In fact, if the Hero Bash was to reproduce with such common breeding stock, it would besmirch the very pride of the orc race.

For all these reasons and more, Bash had decided he would embark to search for his very own bride.

In order to uphold the noble pride and dignity of the orc race.

So the Orc King thought. Nay, it may be more accurate to say that he perceived it, for the Orc King's eye was sharper than any other, as all orcs would agree.

Even though he actually had shockingly bad eyesight.

"You knew..."

Bash lowered his gaze, embarrassed.

He was blushing a deep red. Never would he have expected the king to know the truth. The truth that he was a virgin.

And not only that...the king had used the word *wife*.

The king knew it all...Bash's plans to travel away from this place and lose his virginity in secret, hopefully with a woman who herself was a virgin. Then he would take that woman to wife and practice the act of copulation many, many times.

Yes, Bash was embarrassed.

An orc of his caliber, caught in the act of sneaking off on a trip to lose his virginity.

And to have such a secret discovered by a venerable, much-respected orc like the king, who was something like a father to so many... If he was judged as an embarrassment to the orc race, he could understand it.

In truth, none of that had come out. But Bash, like all orcs, believed that King Nemesis had a keener eye than any in the land and saw all.

"My king, please do not try to stop me. I must—"

"I shall not stop you."

Nemesis raised a hand in the air to quash Bash's excuses.

The king let out a short, self-deprecating laugh, then, narrowing his eyes as if struggling against some inner turmoil, he spoke.

"You may go. I shall say nothing of this to the others."

Nemesis was not without sympathy for Bash.

In fact, as village elder, the king would have offered Bash the chance to take a bride before now, if only the war were still on, and if only the peace treaty hadn't included that pesky clause about not being able to copulate with other races without consent.

If it weren't for that, he would have made sure that Bash lived a lifestyle befitting an orc of his station.

But the war was over. And the peace treaty terms were very clear.

Under such circumstances as these, finding a woman of superior enough quality to serve as wife to an orc like Bash...that would be no simple feat.

For an orc to take a bride without the use of force...such a thing had never been heard of, not in the five thousand years since the war first began.

It would be an extreme challenge, to say the least. A challenge that Bash wished to take on alone. What a man!

For an Orc Hero to set out on a hero's journey...

For him to set out on a journey at all, when in the land of the orcs, he enjoyed every privilege and comfort...

For him to attempt to prove that, despite their defeat in the war, the orcs were still a race worth their pride...

As king, how could he say no to that?

"I thank you."

Bash lowered his head respectfully before the king.

Despite becoming a Hero and earning respect as the strongest of all orcs, never for one moment did Bash dream of going against the king's wishes.

Even though he possessed arguably much greater strength.

Even though, should he and the king fight hand to hand, Bash would probably win.

But there was no kinder or more benevolent orc than the king. To see through to the shameful, weakest part of Bash and somehow not laugh. To give him the time and opportunity to restore his honor. How kind he was to his subordinates, how discreet.

He is truly the king of all orcs. There is no orc more suited to the title. Until my dying day, I shall pledge my fealty to no one else.

As he gazed back at the king, Bash felt surer of this conviction than ever before.

◆

And so Bash set out on his journey.

A long, long journey to lose his virginity...

2
The Fairy

Bash made his way through the forest.

The thick trees tapered to sharp points high above, forming a dense canopy overhead. There were no real paths, only animal trails to be found here and there.

If a human were to attempt to cross these woods, they would be torn to ribbons, lacking the tough skin of an orc. Due to many years on the battlefield, orcs possessed a high level of perception and a finely honed sense of direction.

Bash was headed east to the neighboring country of humans.

The humans were in possession of a larger tract of land than any other race. Not only were they on the winning side as a member of the Alliance of Four, they also won more battles than any other race. Most of the land the orcs had lost had been taken over by the humans.

The orcs didn't bear a grudge against the humans for this, of course. The winner takes the spoils. That was simply a fact of war.

So why was Bash heading to the land of the humans?

Well, the answer is exceedingly simple.

"If you're going to breed, it's got to be a human."

That was one of the sayings the orcs had.

Humans were highly fertile, easy to impregnate, and sturdy, despite the size difference with orcs. And they were also pretty easy on the eyes.

For orcs, humans were the obvious top choice for breeding.

Bash believed so, too.

Ah, I haven't been here in years…

As Bash forced his way through the thick undergrowth, he let his thoughts wander back to the past.

Only three years ago, this forest had been the site of a pitched battle.

It was gone now, but this was where the last stronghold of the orc battalion had been located. The human army's frontline fighters came to force the orcs to capitulate by mounting a massive, head-on attack.

While this was going on, Bash had been hard at work running around the forest, crushing as many human fighters as he could find in an attempt to protect the stronghold.

Thanks to Bash's efforts, they were able to hold out until the end of the war, never giving over the stronghold to the human invaders.

But after the war, the humans seized the stronghold anyway and had it torn down.

In that fight alone, Bash had crushed a large number of human warriors, his final tally numbering in the hundreds.

Many of them were female warriors.

If only he'd taken one of them after, he could have rid himself of his virginity just in time.

But if he had, they might have lost the stronghold. Then again, it was destroyed following their surrender anyway, so what did it even matter in the end?

How ironic it all was.

But if that had happened, then Bash may never have won his title of Hero...

"Hmm?"

As Bash was ruminating over what he could have done differently, he realized he could smell blood on the breeze, coming from far off.

An injured animal, perhaps?

Or perhaps rival wolf packs fighting a turf war among themselves?

"I'd better check it out."

So Bash muttered to himself without hesitation, setting off at a brisk run.

It wasn't mere curiosity that spurred him forward. It was the prospect of finding food.

Hunting down an animal was usually tricky, but if it was already wounded, then it would be losing strength fast, and the fact that it was bleeding meant tracking it by scent would be easy. Wild animals tend to lash out violently when injured, but with Bash's thick hide, no animal fang or claw would do much damage.

During the war, Bash had often captured animals injured from fighting.

"..."

Bash galloped through the forest with the speed and destructive force of a hurricane.

Orcs were known for being lumbering and sluggish, but that wasn't true for Bash. Bash was fleet-footed, known as one of the fastest of the orcs.

And with his tough hide, no overgrown bush nor scraping tree branch could injure him. He was able to propel his wrought-iron body through the hurdle-strewn forest without ever needing to slow down for even a second.

With unbelievable speed, Bash flew toward his destination.

When Bash arrived on the scene, the fight was at its climax.

A horse-drawn carriage with a busted axle was lying on its side just off the narrow path—which was more of a dirt track, really—formed by the wheels of carts passing through. Foodstuffs and other sundry goods were strewn everywhere, and the corpse of a horse could be seen sprawled on the ground.

Two humans were on their feet, both armed with swords, facing off against the enemy.

They were surrounded by bugbears, bearlike beasts that walked on their hind legs. There were six of them.

Bash's eyes narrowed as he quickly took stock of the scene.

Group of bugbears attacked some human merchants, looks like.

It wasn't such an unusual sight. Since the war ended, the world had been at peace, sure, but that didn't affect wild beasts or their natural inclination to hunt humans. Once you left the safety of the towns, you were at the mercies of nature, where survival was a matter of brute strength.

"...!"

"GRAWR!"

As Bash emerged from cover with a rustling of leaves, the bugbears all swiveled their heads in his direction.

Then, while three of them kept their eyes trained on the humans, the remaining three rounded on Bash, fur standing on end, growling ferociously.

Bash never hesitated. Instead, he simply narrowed his eyes at the bugbears.
The next moment, he let out a fearsome roar of his own.

"GRAAAAGH!!!"

It was a war cry.

The same war cry unleashed by all orcs to mark the commencement of battle.

The roar was so loud, it actually shook the trees as it reverberated around the forest. Groups of birds took off from their tree perches in alarm, and the bugbears visibly shivered, furry hides twitching.

"Grawr..."

A simple roar from Bash was all it took to make them understand the obvious—there was no way they could win a fight against the orc standing in front of them.

Losing their will to fight, the bugbears visibly shrank, tails curling around their furry behinds as they turned and fled into the safety of the deep forest. A wild beast can always sense when his enemy is stronger than him.

"Now, then..."

After making sure the bugbears were a safe distance away and not likely to return, Bash turned to the humans left standing next to their ruined carriage.

Whoa...

The humans looked back at him, pale-faced and trembling, clutching their swords. These were *female* humans.

They both looked to be a little past the age of thirty.

Pale, but with healthy, rather appealing bodies. Bash had heard it was best to choose a woman in her late teens when taking one to wife. Any younger, and she wouldn't be ready for bearing children. Any older, and the number of babes she could birth would be limited. But a human in her thirties would do. As long as she could produce offspring, that was all that mattered.

And they're both beauties!

To be frank, neither was what your average orc would consider beautiful, based on conventional orc aesthetic standards.

But Bash had hardly ever seen any women.

To be more precise, he'd actually seen plenty of women, but never from this close up, and he'd never had the opportunity to actually take a good, appraising look at one before.

His first glimpse of human women in the flesh. To Bash, they were dripping with sex appeal to the point where he was afraid he was about to start drooling.

His very first bridal candidates.

After gazing at the women for a few seconds, Bash made up his mind and cleared his throat to speak.

"Ahem. Ladies…would you like to have my babies?"

It was a standard orc proposal.

"Aaaagh!"

"It's going to attack us and…*mate* with us!"

It all happened so fast.

Bash couldn't believe how swift the two were. Why, hadn't they been trembling in shock mere seconds before?

Still clutching their swords, the two women turned tail and fled, leaving everything else they owned lying strewn on the ground.

Unable to bring himself to pursue them, Bash simply stood there, one hand stretched out in front of him, fingers slowly closing in defeat. He cut a forlorn figure.

"…But why?"

Why did they turn him down? Why did they turn and flee? He couldn't understand it.

After he'd rescued them and all…

"This doesn't make any sense…"

Of course, Bash knew that finding a bride wouldn't be so straightforward.

There was never any guarantee he'd be able to actually find a bride.

Reminding himself of the facts, Bash turned sadly to depart.

He was headed once more to his initial destination, the country of the humans.

"Hmm?"

Just then, Bash's keen ears picked up on a strange sound.

It was a dull knocking sound. *Thump, thump.*

Bash cupped his hand around his ear, straining to locate the source of the noise.

The ability to zero in on the subtler sounds…that was a valuable skill to have on the battlefield.

On the night of a new moon, all you had to rely on was your ears and your nose to identify the beastkin unit sneaking up on you with near-silent footsteps.

"…In there?"

The noise was coming from within the carriage.

The carriage that was lying on its side with a broken wheel. Bash approached, following the sound, and began to rummage inside.

"…"

There was nothing much in there.

Just some dried foodstuffs, which the human women must have been sustaining themselves on. And some random tools and household items and things.

No weapons.

They could have at least left me a slave for my troubles… Bash couldn't help thinking that.

"Hmm?"

His keen ears picked up on the dull knocking sound again.

He must have missed something. He began pawing through the wreckage, casting aside things from the mound of random items.

After heaving aside some larger pieces of broken furniture, he realized he could see a faint glow shining from a gap in the debris.

Bash was familiar with the look of that glow. Sighing a little, he plunged his hand into the gap.

When he withdrew his hand, he had a glass bottle clutched in his meaty fist.

The sturdy metal bottle cap had a piece of paper bearing a magic circle firmly attached to it.

The creature inside was about twelve inches tall and bathed in a brilliant glow. Two tiny wings fluttered on its back.

It was a fairy.

"You…"

The fairy looked up at Bash's face with surprise, its little mouth opening and closing helplessly.

It looked like the magic circle paper charm was preventing it from escaping and also from speaking.

Bash peeled off the charm from the bottle cap. The next moment, the cap popped off and went sailing into the undergrowth.

A second later, the fairy came zooming out of the bottle at tremendous speed, flew in a circle around Bash several times, and then attached itself firmly to his face.

"Boss! Long time no see!"

Bash reached up and took hold of the fairy between his thumb and forefinger. It was rubbing and nuzzling itself against Bash's face. Carefully, he pried it off him and held it at arm's length.

Despite the fact that Bash had it firmly caught between his fingers, the fairy didn't seem to mind at all and instead threw its arms open wide, straining toward Bash and clearly intending to give him a hug.

"Oh, Boss! You've saved me! I was starting to think I'd be stuck in that nasty old bottle forever! Oh, even worse! If you hadn't found me, I'd have starved to death trapped under that pile of junk! But you always come through for me, don't you?! ... Hmm? Boss? What's wrong? That look on your face...don't tell me you've forgotten all about me?!"

"How could I ever forget?"

Bash knew this fairy.

The fairy's name was Zell. Their true name was too long to remember, so this shortened moniker sufficed.

During the war, the fairies and the orcs had been battle buddies.

The fairy race is gifted with the ability to fly at incredibly fast speeds and heal wounds with the dust that fell from their bodies. But they are small in stature, and their attack power is limited to the use of wind magic only, which means they aren't really a race built for combat.

So during the war, the fairies cooperated with the orcs, serving as messengers, lookouts, scouts, spies, and healers.

Zell was one of the messenger fairies dispatched to the country of orcs and had often relayed messages, orders, and battle status updates to Bash.

Incidentally, the fairies' choice to join the demon-led Coalition of Seven Races during the war was sparked by the oppression they had suffered at the hands of the humans.

The humans prized fairies as curious little pets and also for their healing properties, and so they traded them for high prices.

At the end of the war, the fairies also signed a peace treaty with the humans. However, many humans still saw fit to capture fairies and keep them as pets for the rest of their lives.

Even with the war over, the fairies were still being oppressed, perhaps even more than ever before.

"By the way, Boss, how did you know I'd been captured?"

"I didn't. It was a coincidence."

"A coincidence?!"

Bash let go of Zell, who zoomed out of the horse carriage and flitted curiously about the scene.

Faster to take a look than wait for an explanation. That was the way of a battle scout, perhaps.

After making sure the horse was truly dead, Zell zoomed back to Bash and began fretfully tugging on his ear.

"Hey, hey, hey! Boss! This is bad! You can't attack a human horse-drawn carriage! It's against peace treaty rules! Against! The! Rules!"

"It wasn't me who attacked it. It was swarmed by a group of bugbears."

"No one's going to believe that, you daft orc! A carriage wrecked, an orc lurking nearby...even the dumbest human's bound to put two and two together and say, *Hey, that orc attacked that carriage!* Now hurry up; we need to get away from here at once! If anyone else happens upon this scene, we'll find ourselves surrounded by the army and chained up before you can say *fairy!*"

The army? Bring it on.

...Is what Bash would have liked to say, but he was on a mission to find a bride in the country of the humans, so that probably wasn't the best idea.

"See?! See what I mean?!"

They both heard the sound at the same time. The clinking and clanking of metal.

Bash knew that sound well from the war. It was the sound of human warriors moving in battle formation, their armor clinking as they went.

Bash quickly leaped into the bushes for cover.

A warrior of Bash's caliber could take down a band of enemy soldiers in a fair fight without even breaking a sweat.

But barging into a battle without knowing who the enemy was could never be considered a wise move.

Bash's objective was simple: to find a human wife.

Yes, he would find a nice virgin, cast aside his virginity with her, and then practice, practice, practice until he had completely mastered all the techniques of the mating act. Then he would return to the land of the orcs, triumphant. This was the victory Bash desired.

Fighting a bunch of human soldiers wouldn't get him any closer to achieving that goal. Even a child could tell you that.

So Bash hid behind cover and silently observed the scene.

Sometimes, a warrior needed to hold firm and secure a good position from which to assess the battlefield.

No orc ever rushed blindly into battle. And Bash was no ordinary orc. He was an Orc Hero, a man of shrewd judgement.

"Not here... But an orc... Yes, I'm sure..."

"...And find it! If it attacks... Yes, yes, go ahead and kill!"

Bash could only catch fragments of the conversation, but the humans seemed awfully worked up over something.

Clearly, they had come to the conclusion that the scene was the aftermath of an orc attack, and they were very angry about it.

Interestingly, the human male who was seemingly in charge appeared to still be quite young and had a high voice.

Young army commanders tend to be reckless. Bash knew this from personal experience. If these humans already believed an orc to be responsible for the carriage ambush, then they would attack Bash on sight without even thinking to ask questions first.

"Boss, what are you gonna do? Beat 'em to a pulp?"

If it came to a fight, Bash could crush these human men easily.

But Bash was an Orc Hero. If he killed these humans, it would cause problems for sure. The backlash might even reach orc territory.

Setting out on this trip had caused a lot of embarrassment for Bash. To cause problems for his people on top of that...

"No, I'll just move on."

"Sure thing, Boss."

Zell nodded in agreement, and the two of them sneaked away from the scene as swiftly as possible.

"So how did you end up captured?"

After walking away from the scene of the carriage wreck for about ten minutes, Bash turned to Zell inquisitively.

Bash had thought that Zell returned to the land of the fairies after the war.

The fairies were preyed upon by the humans, but the land of the fairies was surrounded by towering cliffs.

The humans couldn't get near.

Even if, by some method, they *had* managed to enter fairy country, it still didn't make sense that Zell had been captured by a mere human. Zell was one of the fastest fairies alive.

"Well, about that...fairy country's pretty boring, you know. I may be small, but I have the heart of an adventurer and the wanderlust of an explorer! So I'm out here on a search for things no one has seen before..."

"All right, all right. I think I can guess the rest."

"Ah, Boss, your powers of deduction are as impressive as ever!"

Presumably, Zell had gotten bored and left fairy country of their own accord. Then, while flitting around in a flower bed or something frivolous like that, they were waylaid by a human and forced to huff some potent sleeping drug, or otherwise put to sleep by magic. Then into the bottle Zell went.

Fairies were such ephemeral creatures. Simpleminded humans only ever really managed to get their hands on them through sheer dumb luck.

"Ah, but you know, running into you like this, Boss...what a lucky fairy I am!"

Zell was zooming in excited circles around Bash's head, gushing.

Fairies were capricious, excitable, and mischievous creatures. The more excited they became, the more frenetic their movements.

"Incidentally, Boss, what are *you* doing out here in the forest? I heard they're calling you Hero now back in orc country. Oh, by the way, congrats on the Hero title! An Orc Hero; that's second rung on the ladder from the Orc Elder himself, right? I totally thought you'd be living it up, basking in the admiration of all orckind and having yourself a sweet retirement!"

"..."

"Oh yikes, some jealous orc framed you for something, didn't they? Oh, I know! They framed you in a murder plot to kill the elder! Then all the other orcs had no choice but to cast you out of the village! How tragic! If you're out for revenge, I'll help you! My blade already longs to slit all their throats!"

"Orcs don't get jealous. And the elder is alive and well."

It was true. No orc was ever jealous of one they called Hero.

An orc by that title had already proven himself as indisputably great by the criteria decided upon by all orcs.

How could they be jealous of one they had unanimously decided to respect? Although there was always the odd exception. The possibility of a random flare of jealousy mixed in among the envy.

"So then, what are you doing out here?"

Bash pressed his thick lips together tightly.

He could never tell that he was on a journey to lose his virginity. Zell may have been an old battle buddy, but there were limits to what Bash was willing to share, even with close friends.

"Well, you don't have to tell me if you don't want to! But you know, I owe you my life. You've saved me tons of times on the battlefield, even before just now. Don't you remember? When we first met? I'd been caught by a human warrior. *'Fairies don't need arms and legs! All we need's the fairy dust it drops!'* I thought for sure I was a goner. Then you appeared in a blaze of glory. *'You won't need arms or legs in hell, either.'* That's what you said! Then you actually chopped off all the human's limbs, *whack, whack, whack!* Oh boy, that was quite a sight to see! I fell in love right on the spot! I decided that day that I'd follow you anywhere, Boss! So anyway, our background being what it is and all, I'm here to offer you my services! You're a blockheaded orc, so maybe you don't understand the delicate sensibilities of a brave fairy such as myself."

Zell struck a confident pose, floating in the air in front of Bash's nose. He waved the fairy away, thinking hard to himself. Being honest, he realized he didn't have much knowledge of other races aside from orcs.

In fact, his knowledge only extended to which races were good for breeding with and which ones weren't.

In contrast, Zell had spent the war as a messenger and spy and knew all about the lifestyles of various races.

On top of that, Zell was skilled at gathering intel. Considering the path that lay before him, having someone like Zell along would be a definite asset.

"...I'm looking for a wife."

"A...wife?"

Zell stopped zooming around in circles and came to a full stop.

Then they floated there, deep in thought, staring intensely at Bash's face.

Bash looked away quickly, fearing his secret chastity was about to be sniffed out.

After a long pause, Zell finally became animated again, clapping their tiny hands loudly.

"A wife's a big deal for an orc, ain't it? Of course, an orc of your renown should have a bride. But you ain't gonna find a suitable bride in orc country, things being what they are. So you've set out on a journey to find a bride, right, Boss?"

"Well...something like that."

Zell's conjecture was much the same as the Orc King's had been.

Anyone who knew who Bash was would reach the same conclusion, probably.

And Zell was known as All-Seeing Zell for their powers of perception. It was a nickname they'd given themself, mind you.

"I see, I see... A bride for the boss, eh...? If I weren't a fairy, I'd be volunteering for the role myself..."

Fairies have tiny little bodies.

Clearly, they are wholly unsuited to breeding with other races. What's more, the genders of fairies could not be neatly separated into male and female categories. That's what made them the perfect partners for the orcs in battle.

Simply put, a fairy would never do for a bride.

"All righty, then!"

After thinking it over for a few moments, Zell suddenly struck their chest.

"I've got it! If that's the situation, then leave it to me! At times like this, there probably ain't too many ladies out there who'd like to become the bride of an orc. That might be an issue. But a fine fellow like you, Boss, I bet you can get your pick out of ten...maybe even twenty willing candidates! After all, you're such a catch, even I'd love to be wifed up by you!"

Bash knew well how competent Zell was from the war.

Many times, Zell had infiltrated the enemy camp and brought back vital information.

In fact, Zell's info-gathering skills were second to none among the fairy race. However, Bash also knew that Zell had been captured by the enemy and almost killed many times, too...

But now the war was over. There would be no real danger involved in simply searching for a wife.

What harm could come from relying on Zell's help?

"If it means that much to you, then you can come along."

"Whoo-hoo! Okay then, let's hit up the town! You won't find any beauties lurking about in the deep forest, you know! Watch out, ladies, here comes Bash!"

And so Bash had teamed up once again with his old war buddy, Zell.

An orc and a fairy working together once more.

At a brisk pace, the two of them set off together to the country of the humans.

3

The Fortified City of Krassel

Krassel, the Fortified City.

It had served as the front line of the war against the orcs for centuries.

The majority of the structures were built of stone, and there were blacksmith's forges everywhere belching out smoke.

There were still a lot of rough-looking soldiers to be seen milling about town among the merchants and the regular townsfolk, but not as many as there had been during wartime.

The town sat on top of a small hill and was surrounded by thick, double-rampart walls.

In between these walls sat multiple cannons and trebuchets for self-defense, and there were watchtowers in strategic places around the town from which you could get a good view of the entire forest, the prior dominion of the orcs.

It really was a fortress.

The orcs and humans had clashed over this fortress many times during the war.

Over a period of several thousand years, the orcs repeatedly seized the fortress, only to have it wrested from their grasp by the humans.

The humans had defended the fortress tirelessly. If it fell to the orcs, so too would the entirety of human land. The men would all be killed, the women taken to become broodmares. The humans understood this ever-present threat well. Even with the war over, they never lost their sense of wariness when it came to dealings with the orcs.

In fact, the war had taught them many things.

They had learned that the orcs weren't single-minded beasts driven only by sexual desire. And they had learned that orcs attacked other races because they needed them to breed.

They had their own set of rules, their own unique sense of pride.

Once the humans realized this and began actually engaging in dialogue with the orcs, they found that negotiation was indeed possible.

With that knowledge, the humans were able to succeed at making peace with the orcs.

After developing a sense of respect for the pride of the orcs, the human female warriors, who possessed a strength even the orcs had to appreciate, were able to negotiate with them. Thus, the orcs realized that women of other races could be strong fighters, worthy of respect, and this led to them agreeing to the peace treaty clause which stated that orcs would no longer "*engage in nonconsensual coitus with members of different races.*"

However, seeing that compliance with such a rule would lead only to the eradication of the entire orc race, the humans gathered together criminal women from all across the land and packed them off to the country of the orcs on *voluntary service*. Thus, the humans swiftly removed the last obstacle the orcs had to accepting peace.

As a result, relations were at this point comparatively friendly between the two races. In fact, they had even begun to set up a fledgling trade route between themselves.

However, many humans still held firm to the belief that orcs were wild beasts without any capacity for reason.

Every race has its fair share of idiots, you see.

Contextually, however, the war had only ended a few years prior. Many still held personal grudges against the orcs. And there were also bands of rogue orcs who had abandoned their nation, infiltrated the land of the humans, and routinely attacked them on their home soil.

So you see, perhaps the humans had a good reason to always be on their guard.

"I never expected it would take us *that* long to get into the town."

"You didn't? Aren't all human towns like that?"

Around three hours had passed since Bash had arrived at Krassel.

Of those three hours, one had been spent arguing with the gatekeeper.

The man had reacted with immediate fear and pointed his spearhead at Bash, all because he happened to be an orc.

Zell had quickly zoomed between them, swiftly explaining that Bash was simply a traveler passing through and that he wasn't one of the dangerous rogue orcs. Without Zell, Bash would probably never have been granted access into town.

The gatekeeper wasn't an easy man to convince, though, and he seemed determined that no orc would be permitted through the gates on his watch. But eventually, he had no choice but to relent and let them in. Travelers tended to be welcomed into human towns as a general rule, and there was nothing set in stone to say that orcs were to be denied entry.

"Lots of women about."

"Yeah, 'cause it's a human town."

Bash peered out of the inn's window at the passersby outside, marveling at the sheer number of eligible females.

Even during war, the only time he'd seen this many women was when he'd been teamed up with the succubus army. Although referring to female succubi as *women* probably wasn't the best choice of words...

Incidentally, the women on the street who caught sight of Bash ogling them from the window all immediately stiffened and quickened their gaits, hurrying past the window as fast as they could.

"With this many women around, I'll have my pick of the lot."

"Whoa, not so fast! There, take a look at that human. Left hand, ring finger."

Bash narrowed his eyes, focusing on the woman's hand as instructed.

There was something sparkling there.

"Hmm? The woman is wearing a ring."

"That's a sign she's already married. Humans generally tend to pair up, one man and one woman. So don't go setting your sights on anyone with a ring, got it?"

"But most of the women here appear to be wearing rings."

"That's 'cause humans think marriage is like some rite of passage to being a proper adult. They all think that, men and women both. Once you get past a certain age, they're all married, more or less."

Unlike the orcs, it seemed all human men were free to take a wife.

This generally accepted human social construct struck Bash as deeply odd.

Eventually, though, he realized that if the number of human men and the number of human women were about equal, then it made sense for their society to allow such things.

And if human women were so keen to marry, that could only work in Bash's favor.

"So what I'm saying is that you should specifically seek out women without rings on."

"The human woman I tried to talk to on the way here... I don't believe she was wearing any rings."

"Ah..."

Yes, on the way to the inn, Bash had plucked up his courage and decided to try to talk to a woman on the street. Her response was to flee screaming.

In fact, Bash hadn't even gotten a word out.

All it took was a single look to send her running.

"It looks like there's still a strong sense of prejudice against orcs."

"I see..."

"They think all orcs are out to attack them indiscriminately, bash in the men's heads, and drag the women off kicking and screaming to be impregnated."

"Well, they're not wrong. During the war, that's what all orcs did."

Even though the current Orc King had outlawed such practices.

Rogue orcs aside, no orc would ever attack indiscriminately in peacetime. Decent orcs had all pledged fealty to the Orc King and were all proud, noble warriors.

But Bash knew that not every human held such prejudiced views about orcs.

A group of soldiers had come running in response to the woman's screams.

They didn't seem to be particularly biased against orcs, and after Bash had explained the situation, they actually became quite friendly.

"*If you're a traveler, you'll need a place to stay,*" one had said, and they'd even given Bash a recommendation for a good inn.

The lodgings were comfortable indeed, and Bash felt grateful to the friendly soldiers for the tip.

"All humans have that image of the wartime orc fresh in their minds. It's only been a few years, after all. Naturally, they're still wary of orcs. I wouldn't have expected them to just run away, though."

"Wary...yes... Actually, before I met you, I tried speaking to those two women in the forest. They ran away from me, too."

"Interesting. Out of curiosity, what did you say to them?"

"I asked if they'd like to have my babies."

"Yikes!" yelped Zell, smacking their forehead with the palm of their tiny hand. "You can't just say something like that!"

"I can't?"

"Listen to me. Humans consider giving birth to be a very intense, almost spiritual thing! It's a super-serious ceremonial event!"

"Goodness..."

The words *ceremonial event* made Bash think of the yearly orc ritual of praying to the god of war. Once a year, the grand ceremony would be held to determine the fortunes of the following year's battle. It was a very, very important ceremony for the orcs.

No orc would ever make light of the yearly ritual.

"And usually, humans only marry and mate with a partner they've fallen in love with. Human women don't go around having babies with men they've only just met."

"Th-they don't...?"

Talk about culture shock.

It was no wonder, then, that human females seemed to abhor the prospect of mating with orcs. It wasn't just because orcs were the enemy. It was because, along with defiling their bodies, orcs would be defiling their deeply-held belief system, too.

"So in summation! If you want to make a human woman your bride, first you'll need to make her fall head over heels in love with you!"

Zell wasn't completely correct there.

Of course, not every human marriage was a result of true love. But as far as Zell knew, that's all there was to it.

"Hmm... But I don't know how to make a human female fall in love with me."

Orcs had no concept of love or romance.

They saw females as creatures to be overpowered and subjugated. Now that was outlawed, and Bash instead somehow needed to make one "fall in love" with him. He hadn't the first clue how to go about doing that.

"Just leave it to me! You may be surprised, but I'm actually a font of knowledge when it comes to all things human!"

Zell thumped a tiny fist against their chest as they spoke.

The fairies had specialized in covert messaging and secret intelligence during the war, and they really did possess a good deal of knowledge about different races. And not just about humans, either, but also about the elves and beastkin, in particular.

That said, the extent of their knowledge concerned things like battle tactics, specific behavioral traits, combat methodology, the characteristics of their tracks and droppings, how to identify them in low visibility, and other aspects relating to war. As for the reproductive habits of these races, the fairies picked up a few things from naughty magazines they found discarded along the road or the bawdy banter they overheard in taverns.

"Thank you. I'm lucky I ran into a fairy of your caliber, and so early in my journey, too. So then, in basic terms, what do I need to do?"

"Well, let's see..."

Grinning confidently, Zell hopped up onto the table.

Then the fairy raised one tiny finger in the air, preparing to start the lesson.

"First of all, human women like being clean! If you're dirty or stinky, you won't get anywhere!"

Rule Number One: Keep a Clean Body.

"So I should bathe before I go out hunting for women, then."

"After bathing, you could also put on some of that stuff you splash on before going into battle with the beastkin!"

"But that...won't that just stink even worse?"

"Don't talk gibberish! That stuff smells exquisite!"

Bash looked down at his bulky body, gnawing on his lip.

During the war, the orcs had faced off against several different races. The beastkin were particularly keen-nosed.

The beastkin could sniff out the distinctive odor of an orc from miles away and often were able to launch successful surprise attacks using only smell to guide them.

To circumvent this, the orcs began bathing before battle with the beastkin in order to suppress their natural scent and would even splash on cologne afterward to further fool their adversaries.

The cologne smelled just like natural grasses and flowers and was sure to confuse the nose of even the sharpest beastkin.

The cologne was actually a fairy-made product, currently a popular export to the human and elf regions.

"Look, I'll lend you some of mine!"

"All right."

Rule Number Two: Always Smell Good.

The sweet cologne's scent was very unpopular among orcs. Many opted out of the practice of applying the cologne before engaging in battle with the beastkin. All of them had died.

Bash was not among their number.

No, Bash was one of the few who actually returned home from the beastkin battles.

But he never forgot the terror of a midnight attack from the beastkin.

It was so bad that the orcs could barely sleep at night. Applying the cologne was the only thing that allowed them to sleep without fear.

As long as the cologne remained potent, there was no need to worry that a beastkin scouting party would sniff them out and launch an attack.

"All right, let's get you bathed! I'll scrub your back!"

Zell sprang off the table, did a loop in midair, and then zipped over to the door, knocking on it with a tiny fist.

"Innkeeper! Innkeeper! The boss wishes to bathe! We need a bucket of water in here, pronto!"

There was a pause of several moments after Zell's shout, and then the door finally opened. The innkeeper poked his head through the gap, looking suspicious.

"The *orc* wants to bathe?"

"What, you got a problem with that? Is an orc not *allowed* to bathe?! You humans are always looking down on orcs for being stinky and dirty, but a decent orc like the boss is perfectly capable of bathing when he comes to a human town, so as not to offend your delicate noses!"

"All right, all right, don't get upset. I'll fetch your bucket of water. That'll be one copper coin, please."

"Certainly."

Despite his look of disbelief, the innkeeper accepted the copper coin and immediately disappeared to fetch a bucket of water.

"All right then, until the water gets here, let's continue the lesson!"

"Yes, if you wouldn't mind."

After that, Bash carefully washed himself with water while listening intently to Zell's specialized fairy advice on "how to be popular with human women."

"So anyway, if you make sure to follow those rules, you should be able to charm at least one woman."

"Keep clean, smell good, act dignified, speak wisely..."

After bathing, Bash went over Zell's rules one by one, counting on his meaty fingers.

Bash was always keen to oblige. He'd once even run to help when a call for backup came in on the battlefield, even though he hadn't slept in three days and three nights.

So he listened attentively to Zell's lesson, drinking in the information without any sense of doubt. Even though, as fairies went, Zell was a bit of an oddball.

"..."

All of a sudden, Bash froze.

His sharp ears had picked up on a sudden clamor. As he listened closely, he realized the noise was all around them, encircling the room they were in.

"Oh, crumbs... Look, there's no need to freeze up. Okay, I'll go over the basics again. Now listen here, a human woman is— *Whoa!!!*"

Zell did a double take as Bash swiftly unsheathed the sword from its holder on his back.

"Wh-what are you doing?! Are we under attack?!"

Despite his shock, Zell reacted quickly, whipping out a magic staff the exact length and size of a toothpick.

But then Zell heard it, too.

The sound of clinking metal on metal, all around them.

They were completely surrounded. How could they not have noticed such an ambush?

"Silencing magic..."

Bash recalled the human trick of using magic to conceal their approach and readied his sword.

Silencing magic, as the name suggested, was magic that muffled sound. However, it was only effective on a fixed area. This meant that once the enemy was close enough, their presence would become suddenly audible. It was one of the forms of magic the full-body-armor-clad humans used most often. If Bash and Zell could hear them now, then that must have meant the humans had either accidentally gotten too close, or they had already successfully surrounded them and were ready to launch an attack...

Judging by the sophistication of the ambush, it appeared to be the latter.

"From the sound, I can guess their number. It must be that group I encountered by the carriage."

"You mean we were followed?"

"I didn't sense anyone following us. But these are humans we're talking about. It's very possible."

Bash wasn't some senile, doddery old orc. He'd have had to be to miss a group of humans in heavy armor tailing him in the forest. No, Bash would never make such a mistake. His senses could always pick up on the presence of the enemy, be they human, elf, or beast.

But humans were very skilled at gathering information on an enemy's location from the slightest of clues. It was possible Bash had inadvertently left behind some sort of barely perceptible trail that the humans had been able to follow.

"Boss, what's the plan? To kill 'em all, it would be best to start attacking them from the window, then waylay the rest when they come around to break down the door. To break through them and escape, it would be best to go out through one of the doors that's least heavily guarded. From the sound of their footsteps, they're not on high alert, and it doesn't seem like they're expecting us to attack them from in here. Still, we can handle about this many enemies without even breaking a sweat, I'd wager."

Zell sounded completely calm and unruffled.

The fairy may have looked young and cute, but make no mistake, Zell was a battle-hardened veteran of war.

Pinpointing an enemy's location in a second and determining the most likely direction of an attack—Zell specialized in both.

Bash and Zell had long worked as a team. During the war, the two of them had broken free of ambushes like this on too many occasions to count.

It would take an attack one hundred times more cunning than this to kill Bash.

Yes, this would be a piece of cake.

But even so, Bash shook his head.

"No, we mustn't let this come to blows. We have to settle things with diplomacy."

And then Bash took his hand off his greatsword.

Bash didn't know why they'd been surrounded, but he did know that he had done nothing improper.

"Um, I don't think that will help. They'll just pin the blame on us for whatever they're upset about and run us out of town."

"Perhaps. But if they've tracked me this far, that means they already know I was at the scene of the carriage ambush. Running away won't change that."

As Bash and Zell were still mid-conversation, the door was suddenly kicked in with an explosive crashing sound.

"Hold it right there, orc!"

Three people leaped into the room.

Two of them were foot soldiers dressed in basic armor, but the third was a knight, wearing a helmet with a horsehair plume on top.

From Bash's many years of battle experience, he instantly recognized the plume helmet as the raiment of a knight.

He also knew that a human knight was the equivalent of an orc war chief.

In other words, the knight was the leader of this detachment.

"I'm not going anywhere! What do you want with me, human?"

"Hmph!"

The knight took several steps into the room and then tugged off his helmet.

A shining golden ponytail whipped free of the helmet. She was, in actuality, a beautiful woman and not a man at all.

I thought that was a high-pitched voice I heard. So it was a woman after all... Ah, but not just any woman...

As Bash looked upon her face, something inside his chest seemed to swell.

A sensation of exquisitely sharp sweetness seemed to flood his entire being, like biting into a ripe fig bursting with juice.

She's incredible...

Dignified brows, a strong-willed mouth, almond-shaped, slightly cruel eyes, translucent, pale skin...

It was hard to make out due to the armor she was wearing, but Bash could tell from the way she carried herself that she had a sturdy, well-muscled body, with broad hips.

This woman was a cut above the ones he'd seen in the forest and the one he'd tried to speak to in town. No, several grades above.

The possibility that he and this beautiful woman might get naked and have intercourse together sent an electric shock straight to Bash's brain.

All of the blood in his body seemed to rush straight to his crotch.

Luckily, however, his sturdy leather undershorts managed to conceal his excitement.

The woman narrowed her eyes at Bash and began snapping at him in a loud voice. Had she noticed his reaction? Perhaps.

"We got a report that an orc attacked a carriage on the road. That was *your* doing, wasn't it?!"

"See? What'd I tell ya?" whispered Zell, but Bash paid no heed. He was suddenly desperate to get this lovely knight to like him.

She was the finest human woman specimen Bash had ever seen. If a group of orcs was to get together as buddies and discuss their *ideal* wife candidate, a beauty like this knight would be in the running for sure.

A virgin like Bash couldn't help being instantly entranced.

His thoughts had already leaped directly to marriage.

He'd want at least three children from her, if not more.

Indeed, elf lore says that when an orc mates with and impregnates a human, sometimes a non-orc is born. Bash wouldn't mind if one of his offspring was a human.

All he asked was that they were all boys, please.

He would name the first son Ash, as a tribute to himself. He would teach him all about fighting and hunting...

"Are you some kind of idiot?! Answer me already!"

Bash's fantasy was suddenly shattered by the sound of the lady knight's harsh voice.

Forced to confront reality, Bash thought hard about what he should do next.

Firstly, he already knew that asking her to be his bride right off the bat wouldn't work. She would only turn him down. Zell's lesson from before had taught him that.

So what to do, then?

Ah yes. In a situation like this, it would be prudent to examine the lady's left hand. If she wore a ring, then that would signify she was already married and could not be his.

"..."

The lady knight's left hand was covered by a gauntlet, and so he could not tell if she was wearing a ring on her finger or not.

"...Hmm."

Bash was stumped. The first lesson he'd committed to memory did not seem to be serving him well.

But he was a noble Hero with years of battle experience.

An enemy that he could not fell with a single stroke of the sword—he had encountered more of those than there were stars in the sky.

Indeed, he had once spent countless hours in combat with a beastkin behemoth. They had fought from sunup to sundown.

Sometimes, you needed to thoroughly take stock of an enemy's power, drawing the battle out to last many hours.

"Answer me, damn you! I refuse to let an *orc* waste my precious time!"

"Ahem, I apologize... I did indeed see the carriage, only it was not I who attacked it. I simply spoke up afterward, but the survivors fled..."

Bash remained calm and answered her evenly, as a proud orc warrior should.

That was another one of the "how to be popular with human women" rules Zell had taught him.

Rule Number Three: Act Dignified and Manly.

"Don't lie to me!"

"I'm not lying. I saw the carriage being besieged by bugbears. I was simply passing by, so I chased off the bugbears."

"And do you have any proof of that?"

"I have none. But I swear it is true, on the name of the Orc King, Nemesis!"

"Huh?"

The knight seemed visibly staggered by Bash's proud declaration.

Swearing on the Orc King's name was very serious. To do so in support of a lie was a crime punishable by death.

The only orcs who could make such a claim were the most exalted of all warriors, greater than the greatest of war chiefs.

In other words, it was a declaration uttered only by the manliest, most noble and honorable of orcs.

Such an orc, upon making this kind of proclamation, would be sure to receive looks of admiration from the younger orcs and would be taken very seriously indeed.

Bash gazed at the surprised-looking knight, smiling internally. *That takes care of that!* he told himself.

But the female knight knew nothing of the orc customs.

Her discomfort came from the difficulty she was now facing in continuing to assign blame to such a *brazen liar* of an orc.

"The survivors said an orc approached them and attempted to *impregnate* them."

"The practice of mating with other species without consent has been outlawed by the Orc King. I was simply checking to see if I had their consent."

"There's no way they'd ever consent to doing *that* with *you!*"

"I knew I had to ask first, and so I did. I later learned that in human culture, it is very difficult to obtain consent when requesting to mate with a woman shortly after meeting her."

The knight blinked wildly at the orc, who continued to speak of ridiculous things in such a cool, prideful manner.

She had never met such a confident, well-spoken orc in her life.

The only orcs she'd ever known were the rogue ones who'd been cast out of their own country.

Those rogue orcs, upon setting eyes on the female knight, would immediately start threatening to violate and impregnate her, using the foulest language. Then, upon being questioned, they would dissolve into boiling fits of rage.

She'd never even been able to have a civilized conversation with an orc before.

"You... You dirty, good-for-nothing orc! Fine, so you were just passing by... But you forgot to mention that you ransacked the carriage before you left!"

"Hmm..."

The lady knight's accusation had Bash in a bind.

It was true he had taken something from the carriage. Although, to be precise, it was not some*thing* he had taken, but rather some*one*...

"Indeed, I did retrieve—"

"So you admit it! I'm arresting you for theft!"

"Hmm..."

"J-just hold on a minute, will ya?"

Zell zoomed in between Bash and the knight and hovered there in the air.

"You're talking about me, right? Yes, I was in the carriage! Poor me! Captured and bottled by humans! But you know, it's totally forbidden for humans to capture fairies and trade them like slaves! I was smuggled goods! And all this fine orc did was rescue me. Now you're arresting him for theft? Where's the justice?!"

"Wh-what?"

The knight looked deeply concerned.

Fairy smuggling was indeed a serious crime. So the carriage was transporting a captured fairy, and the orc had rescued it. But theft was still theft, whether the goods had been smuggled or not, right? In fact, wouldn't this mean the orc was actually guilty of being in possession of stolen goods?

But it seemed like the fairy had decided to accompany the orc of its own free will.

There was no guarantee the fairy was even telling the truth, though. Perhaps it was spinning her a yarn? Fairies made up stories as naturally as they breathed.

"Uh..."

The situation had become entirely too complicated.

The knight bit her lip, eyes darting back and forth as she mulled it all over. Then she made up her mind.

"At any rate, you're going to come with us!"

"Sounds good to me," Bash responded without even blinking.

Zell was the one who was surprised. Turning in midair, the fairy gazed at Bash, perplexed, jerking a thumb over their shoulder at the knight and then flailing their limbs questioningly. The knight also seemed shocked by how easily Bash had agreed to accompany her.

"Are you *sure* about this, Boss? She's being awful disrespectful to you!"

Generally speaking, an orc would never agree to go along with the enemy quietly.

If Bash had been given the same order back in the orc country, he'd have whipped out his sword, bared his tusks, and growled *Bring it on!* before you could say *orc*.

But Bash had his trip's objective to think about.

Discarding his virginity.

Preferably, with a woman he found attractive. And if she was a virgin, too, then all the better.

"I'm happy to oblige!"

Bash considered the woman in front of him.

A blond, spirited-looking female knight. Beautiful and definitely his type. But he didn't know if she was a virgin or not. Or if she was married. But despite the look of distaste on her face as she glared at him, she hadn't yet run off screaming.

No, in fact...she wanted him to go with her.

If he did, then at least that would give him more opportunity to engage her in conversation.

If he refused to go, then their acquaintance would end here. Violence would ensue, and if he ended up being driven from the town, then he would probably never see her again.

When he weighed it all up like that, there was no good reason to deny her request.

In battle, you often only got one chance to make it back alive.

Until now, Bash had never missed a single one of those chances. He was quick to make up his mind.

"F-fine, then. Put him in handcuffs! We're taking him away!"

"Hmm..."

And so Bash allowed himself to be arrested.

Only four hours had passed since he first made it to Krassel, and already things had taken a rather dramatic turn.

4

The Knight Army General, Houston

Houston was the leader of Krassel's Order of Knights.

He had a long and interesting history.

Around twenty years prior, Houston had entered his first battle as an apprentice foot soldier. He was only thirteen years old. Sent straight to the front line of battle on his first day in the war, he experienced a bloody defeat. His entire platoon was wiped out, but miraculously, Houston survived. Following that, he fought in countless battles, and within the space of ten years, he became a commander.

His first battle as a commander had been a complete disaster. Just getting back alive was like walking through the flames of hell.

It was a truly terrible battle.

All the officers in charge, from the general to the battalion commander, were either killed or fled the battlefield. With the chain of command changing by the moment, the troops were in a state of complete confusion and turmoil. When around 60 percent of the troops had already been lost, command fell to Houston, then just a lower-ranking troop commander.

"There's nobody left who ranks higher than you."

When his orders were delivered by a combat medic, Houston had been sure it was someone's idea of a bad joke.

But as it transpired, Houston was born for the role.

He rallied his troops and managed to withdraw with only minimal losses among the 40 percent of soldiers left standing.

Houston had found his calling. It was like he was destined to command a great army.

Even though his miraculous safe withdrawal from battle had been more or less a matter of sheer luck...

Regardless, this deed won him the respect of his people, and he was assigned the position of Orc Response Force lieutenant. The Orc Response Force mainly fought against the orc-fairy alliance.

Five years after Houston had become a lieutenant in this division, the general was killed. Houston automatically succeeded him as general and continued to fight until the war ended.

In other words, Houston spent ten years of his life continuously fighting the orcs.

Houston devoted his entire being to the war effort.

He gathered as much information on orcs as he could and educated himself as much as possible. Many times, he risked his life on the front lines of battle.

As a result, he racked up more orc kills than any other human.

And so the humans gave him an honorary title.

That title was Houston the Pig Slayer.

Even after the war, Houston remained on high alert when it came to all things orc related.

He was especially fierce whenever he encountered a rogue orc. He would execute them without even listening to what they had to say, his ears deaf to their screams as they pleaded for their lives. Seeing this, the young folk who had become soldiers after the war viewed Houston with equal parts respect and fear.

Yet despite his incredible nickname of Pig Slayer, Houston's feelings about orcs were extremely neutral.

He was not prejudiced against them. He did not discriminate against them. He did not hate them.

The reasoning for this was that Houston *knew* orcs.

In his ten years of battle, he had become something of an expert on them.

After he became a lieutenant, he'd made it his business to learn everything he could about orcs. This was necessary in order to kill them more successfully and to reduce the number of human casualties.

During those wartime years, Houston had studied up on orcs until he knew more about them than anyone else. He would observe their movements, read up on their history, and even question orc prisoners of war.

Thus, Houston learned.

He learned that orcs had their own moral code and customs, known only among themselves, and that they were proud warriors.

But Houston never came to admire or even soften his heart toward orcs.

No, these beings had slain many of his friends and compatriots. His feelings toward the orcs were dark and complex.

But the war was now over, and he respected the orcs enough that he felt no need to bear a grudge.

His harsh treatment of the rogue orcs was down to them being the scum of orckind.

They refused to abide by even the most basic of orc laws and chose to live in pure selfishness. They intruded into the land of the humans and still refused to respect their rules.

Those who could not conform to the laws of society were no better than wild beasts.

Even worse, they killed indiscriminately.

At any rate, after the war, Houston was promoted to knight and was immediately nominated to be the leader of the Krassel Order of Knights.

With Houston at the helm, another war with the orcs seemed an unlikely prospect, at least for many years to come. Even if another war did happen, the plan was to protect Krassel with everything they had.

"What's that? Have you apprehended a suspect in the highway ambush case?"

One of his subordinates had come to him with this news out of the blue.

"Yes. It appears to be an orc."

"A rogue orc? Didn't I tell you to just have all the rogue orcs killed?"

Houston frowned, displeased by the messenger's tale.

Houston had special permission from the Orc King to execute rogue orcs at will.

He would have preferred it if the orcs would step up and do the job themselves, but they had their own set of societal rules. So Houston had no alternative.

"Um, well apparently, this orc was very well-spoken and clean-cut. It doesn't seem to be a rogue orc at all."

"Then release the poor fellow."

"Um, about that... Judith had some reservations, and..."

"Damn that whelp. If she sparks another war with the orcs, she'll wish she'd never been born..."

Judith was the knight in charge of investigating the highway ambush case.

She was a rookie knight who had only been on the job for a year. At long last, she had finally been entrusted with a mission of her own. It was the kind of mission that should have been wrapped up almost immediately, but there had been no leads. Either the criminal was far craftier than had been expected, or Judith really was that useless.

Recently, Judith herself had been increasingly panicked by her lack of results.

She was desperate to do anything she could to prove she wasn't entirely useless.

"Well, what do you think?"

"Um, well... Judith is right. There are a lot of strange factors at play here. The orc refuses to tell us the purpose of his travel, and he also has a fairy with him. Neither seemed at all concerned to find themselves surrounded by our platoon. If you ask me, I think they might be...spies."

"Pfft!"

Houston snorted dismissively.

This soldier was young and hadn't even been in the war.

So he knew nothing of the orc race.

Anyone with basic knowledge of the orcs could tell you that coming across an orc spy would be like finding a needle in a haystack. As a rule, they didn't exist. Orcs just weren't suited to espionage.

"Lord Houston, this is no laughing matter! No doubt they allowed themselves to be arrested by us so they could gather intel on us from within!"

"Fool! An orc would never be so ingenious. If spying was the objective, the fairy would have come alone."

From all Houston knew of orcs, they would never *allow* themselves to be captured.

If it was intel they really wanted, then the orc would have fought every enemy to the death, whether he had backup or not. Then he would have thrown Judith to the floor and extracted the required information from her through means of carnal torture.

An orc would never be capable of the kind of subterfuge needed to infiltrate an enemy camp and gather intel from within.

Sending a scout ahead was about the extent of an orc's advance preparations.

Getting the measure of an enemy's position, estimating the number of warriors and how they were armed—how many swords, how many bows—and so on...yes, the orcs often scouted ahead, just like other races.

Indeed, while they lacked any prowess in spying, the orcs actually had a wide repertoire of secret battle tactics, the likes of which would make any human's head spin.

But this orc had capitulated and allowed himself to be captured—from that alone, it was clearly impossible that they had a rogue orc on their hands.

No, this was a rational orc, capable of abiding by the Orc King's rules and making nice with humans. And yet Houston had never heard of an orc traveling alone. Orcs were a highly sociable, tribal race. Still, he supposed every race had its outliers. An orc traveling alone wasn't really so shocking.

No, Judith had merely panicked and detained an innocent orc. That seemed to be the extent of the situation.

At least, that was the conclusion Houston had already come to.

But it is odd that he's apparently being accompanied by a fairy.

During the war, orcs and fairies had worked together. Did this mean the two of them were engaged in some sort of combat operation?

Even though the war was over, Houston was always on alert for the faintest whiff of discord on the air.

"All right, I suppose I'll simply have to go and take a look for myself."

Houston slapped his knees before getting to his feet.

The jail was located in the basement of the Order of Knights HQ.

During the war, its cells had been filled to the brim with POWs, who were often tortured to death for information. During the last months of the hostilities, a plague spread among the prisoners. Houston had always refused to set foot in the place.

Post-war, though, the jail had been fully cleaned, and now it was mostly used to detain minor offenders.

These days, it was so clean that even a faint hint of citrus wafted on the air.

"Just cut the crap already and tell us the reason for your journey! Why were you walking through the forest? What are you doing in Krassel? And what the heck is with the fairy?!"

As Houston descended the stairs to the jail, he could hear Judith yelling.

Wow, she was really going for the all-out intimidation method. Unexpected of a rookie knight.

How was a captured orc supposed to speak openly in the face of such hostility?

Orcs loathed being looked down on by anyone. Being looked down on by a *woman* was probably more than they could stomach.

Your average orc's sense of pride would never permit him to crack under the interrogation of a woman, even if he had nothing to hide.

Houston smiled dryly.

This was surely the cue for the orc to bark: *If ya wanna know so bad, ya gonna hafta beat it outta me!*

If things got that far, then the interrogation as a whole would be a lost cause.

Judith's approach was absolutely the worst possible mode of interrogation for an orc.

"The objective of my journey is a private matter. In short, I am in pursuit of something. I was walking through the forest, as that is the fastest route. And I have come here because I believe what I seek is likely to be found here. As for the fairy, they're a friend. They are aware of my objective, and they have come along to assist me."

The orc's response was calm and firm. How unusual.

Houston gave a snort of amusement. A passionate, hot-blooded orc would inevitably explode under questioning. But the more established ones, the veteran warriors—there seemed to be more of them about after the war. They were much harder to rattle.

Their senses were perhaps dulled by the sound of so much roaring and bellowing during battle. A mere interrogation may have sounded like a pleasant conversation to them.

But if this was a veteran warrior orc, then that raised further questions.

Why would such an orc be wandering the lands outside of his own country, searching for *something?*

"What is this thing you're looking for? And why do you need it?!"

"That...I refuse to say."

"Why?! That's highly suspicious! What are you hiding, you wretched orc?!"

Perhaps something that, if identified, may be at risk of being stolen?

Or could it be something the orcs had lost that they did not wish the other races to know was lost? Houston weighed these two possibilities in his mind. He had reached the jailhouse door now, but all of a sudden, a deep, dark sense of foreboding washed over him.

That voice...haven't I heard it somewhere before?

Houston's intuition was correct.

He had always placed a great deal of faith in his hunches, and as a result, he had always come back alive from the battlefield.

Actually, I don't think I'll go in there after all...

He often got this prickly sensation in his chest when he was faced with certain dangerous situations. The sensation would come and go, like an internal whisper, keeping Houston safe from harm.

But even if his senses were telling him to withdraw, this was peacetime. There was no threat to his life waiting for him down in that jail cell.

Besides, if he left Judith to her own devices, it would only prolong this pointless interrogation. If there was one thing Houston really hated, it was wasting time.

So Houston carried on, opening the door to the interrogation room.

"Judith, don't overdo it. If you turn this into a diplomatic issue, it will be... *Eeeek!*"

Houston let out a cowardly scream.

He felt a tingle running down his spine, and his heart began to hammer against his ribcage. He was overtaken by an immediate urge to run.

All of a sudden, his mind was back on the battlefield, a battle that had taken place shortly after he was appointed general of the Orc Response Force.

The battle should have been an easy win for them.

They had the greater power, the craftier tactics.

But despite that, their vanguard was unable to break through the enemy line. Their squad was scattered by a surprise sidelong attack. While their reserve platoon then rushed to the front line, their main unit had been besieged by orc warriors.

Had the orcs predicted their battle plan? Or had it all just been a coincidence? The orc brigade that had besieged their main unit had been composed of their best warriors. The sight of one orc in particular was burned into Houston's mind. He could see him on the front line whenever he closed his eyes, swinging his mighty sword.

That orc killed the Response Force's lieutenant, a proud soldier.

While the lieutenant was in the process of being slain, Houston had retreated as fast as his legs could carry him, gasping for breath. He managed to make it back to base safely, but the battle had been like something out of a nightmare. He'd never quite gotten over the trauma of it.

It wasn't a nightmare, though.

Because it kept on happening after that.

Houston encountered that same orc over and over again on the battlefield. Maybe it was just his imagination, but Houston always got the feeling the orc was trying to kill him in particular.

Maybe the orc *was* targeting him. He was the general, after all, and if he was slain, the battalion as a whole would be weakened.

Houston had never engaged in direct combat with that orc, however.

He always ran from every encounter, as fast as his legs would carry him. Even so, it was a miracle he'd managed to escape with his life each time.

The orc would show himself on even the most grueling battlefields.

No matter how strong and numerous the human army, the orc always showed up. And he would always fight to the last man standing.

At the battle of Remium Plateau, for instance, the wise human elders had the ingenious idea to bring a dragon onto the battlefield. And while this dragon turned the demons and ogres into charcoal, the orc stood firm, continuing to fight the dragon along with his surviving comrades.

Houston couldn't help admiring the orc as he watched him in battle.

Indeed, there was something about the hideous orc's skill that made him seem almost beautiful to Houston.

That's why the memory of that particular orc had stuck with him.

Ordinary green orc skin. The standard large tusks, though still a bit small for an orc. A brawny, muscular physique.

Eyes like a hawk. Purplish-bluish hair.

His appearance was unremarkable, that of any green orc, but Houston knew he was not mistaken.

The last time he'd been this close to him, it was at the peace treaty signing ceremony.

No, he wasn't this close even then. There must have been at least sixty-five feet of space.

But the orc standing before him now was a mere sixteen feet away.

Close enough to grab him.

He apparently wasn't carrying that sword of his, the one that was as long as he was tall. But Houston knew...

Yes, Houston knew the orc was capable of moving at speeds that would match even the wild beastkin race and that he could pulverize dwarven black-steel armor with only his bare hands.

He'd seen these feats with his own two eyes, after all. He was not mistaken.

Nobody had quite believed him when he'd told the tale later, but that was how the last adjutant had been killed.

Yes, this was an orc worthy of all the titles the people assigned to him.

The Mad Warrior, the Destroyer, the Annihilator, the Raging Bull, Steel Arm, the Nightmare of the Shiwanashi Forest, the Green Disaster, the Dragon Decapitator...

There were many more...but all of them were an accurate summary of this fearsome orc.

And in the country of the orcs, they called him...

The Orc Hero Bash.

Houston was in the presence of the most fearsome specimen to be found among the entire orc race.

"..."

On closer inspection, Houston noticed the fairy. It looked to be the same one that had always accompanied Bash on the battlefield, but right then, it was wrapped up tight in a rolled napkin, lying helplessly on the table.

Houston knew all about this fairy, too.

Fairies have valuable healing properties, so they're rarely ever killed once they've been captured. Knowing this, this particularly shrewd fairy often allowed itself to be captured on purpose so that it could, through some unknown magical means, transmit the humans' positions to the most dangerous orc and call him right to the spot.

As a result, this fairy had earned itself the nickname of Fake-Bait Zell.

"J-Judith..."

Despite his tremulous voice, Houston was somehow managing not to turn tail and run screaming. His subordinates were watching, you see.

Houston was the general of the armed forces. He commanded both knights and foot soldiers alike. He was proud of this and the respect he received from his troops. There was no way he was about to throw away their trust.

Besides, it actually looked like Bash was cooperating with Judith, a mild, calm expression on his face.

His hunter's eyes shone with a sort of warm light as he nodded along to Judith's interrogation like a benevolent old man listening indulgently to the babbling of a young child.

How unexpected. So this demonic killer had a softer side to him. He wasn't all anger and violence. And why would he be? The war had ended. This was peacetime, wasn't it? Yes, even the orc's eyes spoke of peace.

But he was still Bash. The Bash of whispered, fearful legend.

Houston took a deep breath to center himself. Then, with extreme caution, and keeping as much distance between himself and the orc as possible, he turned to deal with Judith.

"What...? Just what is it you're doing here?"

"Sir! We received reports of an orc ambush in the western forest region. Upon investigation, we discovered that an orc had been seen recently entering the town. We tracked him down and arrested him at the inn he was staying in. Right now, I am conducting an interrogation!"

"Ah. Hmm..."

Houston immediately knew this was an arrest based on misidentification.

Bash would never leave any eyewitnesses alive after an ambush. And if he was at all guilty of this crime, he would simply have broken free of the arrest, killing whoever stood in his way and fleeing.

An orc of this caliber could escape with ease, even if he was surrounded by a hundred soldiers.

As to how Houston could think this with such conviction... Well, he'd seen Bash break free of his own troops that way during the war.

"He's given up most of the information, but he still won't tell us the purpose of his journey. Hey, you! Spit it out, you filthy warthog!"

Judith grabbed Bash by the collar and pushed her face up against his, eyes flashing menacingly.

Houston shuddered with sudden terror.

"Ah, don't do that! Stop! No violence!"

He wanted to sound commanding, but his voice came out in an awkward shriek.

Peacetime though it was, who could blame the orc for being angered by this interrogation? Here he was, accused of a crime, dragged down to the jail, and now some wet-behind-the-ears rookie knight who hadn't even been in the war was harassing and disrespecting him.

Yes, Bash had every right to be angry. Furious, even.

"I have nothing further to say."

But Bash didn't appear to be even slightly perturbed.

Instead, he merely twitched his nose, his expression serene.

Perhaps the citrus fruit scent wafting through the jail was having a calming effect on him? Orcs would eat anything, but surprisingly, they had a special appetite for fruit.

Houston felt a rush of gratitude toward the soldier who had suggested freshening up the jail with citrus fruit oil. Perhaps he would even give them a raise.

"Ahem... Judith. Let go of him at once, then step back here with me. *Slowly.*"

"What...? What's wrong with you? What happened to *Houston the Pig Slayer?* Why are you acting so feeble and—?"

"Do *not* address me by that name!"

An orc would surely find Houston's nickname insulting...

Whenever his nickname was mentioned around the rogue orcs they brought in, it always caused a stir. The orcs would become very abusive indeed. *"So you're the one they call Pig Slayer! I'll rip out your guts!"*

That's how much weight the name Pig Slayer carried among the orcs.

Or maybe it was just that they didn't take kindly to being called pigs. Hard to say for sure.

"But, sir, this pig of a rogue orc needs to know who he's dealing with here—the great Houston! Listen, orc-hog. This man is General Houston, and he slayed more orcs than any other during the war! Yeah, while orcs like you sat around picking your foul noses, he—"

Houston suddenly let forth a scream.

"Shut up! Shut your mouth or I'll shut it for you! Now get back in line this instant!"

Houston's roar sounded almost demonic.

"Huh...?"

Judith stiffened with shock, bewildered by Houston's threat. Nevertheless, she did as she was told.

Her shoulders were slumped, her head drooping. She'd been scolded by the army general but had no idea why. She would need him to explain later on.

Right now, though, there was the orc to worry about.

"Whew..."

Houston let out the breath he'd been holding and turned back to Bash.

Bash had his hawklike eyes fixed on Judith, now standing in her position in line. Houston's lip twitched spasmodically.

"I... I apologize for the rudeness of my subordinate. She's supposed to be in charge of investigating the carriage ambush case, but so far, she's failed to find any leads. I'm afraid she's grown a bit desperate. Oh, excuse me, I should have introduced myself earlier. I am the army general of this town's defense force. My name is Houston Jale."

"Bash."

"Ah yes... I know your name..."

"You know of me?"

"I had the opportunity to observe you on the battlefield many times..."

Bash suddenly leaned in, eyes focusing on Houston's face. Would he remember him and leap forth to attack? No, surely not. He was a reasonable sort of orc, wasn't he?

Houston had to trust his initial impression. If the orc was going to attack, he would have already done so. His men would all have been slain, and Judith would have been left lying in a dead faint, eyes glazed over, cloudy liquid dripping from in between her spread legs.

Reassuring himself, Houston manufactured a smile.

In his thirty years of loyal service, Houston had never smiled at an orc this way.

Hell, he'd never even smiled at another human this way.

"A great chief of the humans..."

"Um...sure. Something like that."

"This takes me back to the war... How have you been?"

Suddenly, Bash's tusks were fully exposed.

It was an expression that could easily be mistaken for a threatening grimace. But Houston knew more about orcs than anyone around. He knew that savage expression was simply an orc's approximation of a friendly smile.

Houston felt slightly relieved and much more confident as he continued the conversation.

"This situation is entirely a result of my lack of attentiveness. I very much appreciate your patience during this matter."

"Oh, I'm not bothered at all."

Actually, Bash almost seemed bored, but he was looking at Judith with an odd expression on his face.

Houston narrowed his eyes. *Does this orc mean*, he thought to himself, *that as much as Judith's impudence enrages him, he does not intend to kill her...?*

That was the conclusion Houston came to, at least.

He was a tolerant orc, to be sure, taking Judith's insults on the chin without batting an eye.

Any other orc would have already handled the insult by seizing Judith and tearing her limb from limb.

And yet the orc could still blow his top at any second.

Houston raised his voice, hoping to wrap up this conversation as soon as possible.

"Um... At any rate, may I ask you a few questions? I promise not to take up too much more of your time."

"What? Just how many times do you intend to make me repeat the same thing?"

"Please, if you would just cooperate with us for a few minutes more...!" squeaked Houston.

He shot Judith a sharp look. Was that what her interrogation had amounted to—endless repetition of the same questions?

Judith quickly looked down at the floor, chewing her lip out of guilt.

"Well, let's see..."

Then Houston proceeded to question the orc about the ambush in the western forest region they'd received reports on.

Naturally, Bash's answers did not change.

The carriage had been besieged by bugbears. Bash, who was simply passing by, had stepped in to drive them off.

He had spoken to the two women to see if either would consent to intercourse. And his explanation for why he had not simply pounced on them was that the Orc King had forbidden mating with other races without first obtaining consent.

While Bash had merely been complying with the Orc King's wishes, the women had seen it as a sign that they were about to be attacked.

Houston nodded sagely as he digested this information. Those rogue orcs couldn't be trusted, but he found he could easily believe Bash.

It looked like he really did just happen upon the carriage ambush by pure coincidence.

Yes, Houston had predicted as much.

If he really had meant to attack those two women, they would never have been able to escape to tell the tale. Houston knew better than anyone else that fleeing from Bash was a near-impossible feat. To get away from Bash when he really meant to capture you...that would require countless heavily armored subordinates to use as convenient human shields. Not to mention a good deal of luck as well.

Therefore...

"Just one more question, then."

This was the most important question of all.

"You said you're searching for something. Is the Orc King aware of this?"

"Of course."

"I see."

Now Houston's curiosity was satisfied.

He knew why Bash was here.

He knew the purpose of his journey.

He was on a mission from the Orc King. Nemesis had given Bash a direct order. Obediently, Bash had set out on the Orc King's quest.

The command? *Go forth and search for this object/person.*

"Oh dear, that's quite troubling. In that case, you really should have gone through the proper governmental channels..."

"It is a personal matter. I do not intend to cause trouble."

And yet it was something he felt the need to conceal from the humans. Or some*one*.

It must have been something very important indeed to have an orc of Bash's caliber sent after it.

Something that, once obtained, would lead to great profit for the orcs. Or conversely, something that would lead to great losses if they could not obtain it...

At any rate, it was clear that the orcs placed a great deal of value on whatever it was.

Otherwise, they would never have sent their finest orc out into the world alone.

Houston supposed he had this mysterious mission to thank for Bash not tearing him and Judith limb from limb.

Human carnage could have really upped the difficulty of Bash's mission.

But Houston was desperately curious to know what it was Bash sought...

"All right. I understand the situation."

Houston had decided to ponder Bash's mission no further.

He only hoped this *thing*, whatever it was, wasn't something that might cause harm to the human race.

"Well, that's all we needed you for. I apologize for taking up your valuable time."

No, it was none of Houston's business.

Getting involved, sticking his neck in where it didn't belong...that could prove dangerous. Life-threatening. No thanks.

On the battlefield, there was nothing more precious than human life. At the same time, there was nothing more expendable...

Bash's arrest was a simple case of mistaken identity. He had come along quietly and cooperated with their inquiries, more or less.

As far as Houston was concerned, this matter was dealt with.

Case closed.

Of course, Houston would send a message ahead to the homelands, warning them that the Orc Hero Bash had been by, looking for something. But after that, whatever happened...that was somebody else's problem.

"Hmm."

Bash nodded mildly, starting to unfurl Zell from the bindings that had been used to restrain the tiny fairy.

"Take care on your journey and be careful not to leave any belongings behind."

Houston breathed a sigh of relief as he spoke these parting words to the orc.

Finally, the orc was leaving. Seeing him up close and talking to him, he had to admit that Bash really was a fine figure of an orc and well worthy of the Hero title.

But an orc like that could go on a wild rampage at any moment.

Houston knew much about the orcs. Enough to know that there was plenty more he did not yet know.

He had to get this orc out of here before something set him off and sent him into a rage. After that, all he could do was pray the orc wouldn't cause destruction in the town.

He wouldn't send soldiers after the orc to monitor him. No, his subordinates' lives were precious. He would adopt an entirely hands-off approach.

That was what Houston decided.

Houston's intuition had kept him alive this far. He refused to risk his neck now, when peace was finally here.

"Hmm..."

As Bash unbound the fairy, though, he was frowning.

And he kept glancing at Judith every few seconds.

Huh?

Houston watched Bash sneaking furtive peeks at Judith. Something was setting his intuition senses tingling again.

Bash was free to leave, and yet he was lingering.

What could be the reason? Why was he looking at Judith? Did he still bear a grudge against the knight? But only moments before, Bash had claimed not to have been all that bothered by her interrogation. So why, then, did he seem so fixated on her? What dirt did he have on Judith?

She was a knight. She conducted a search in the western forest region. The road... in other words...

The gears began turning in Houston's head, leading him right to the most logical conclusion.

"Could it be that the carriage ambush case is somehow connected to this thing you seek?"

"...?"

Bash froze for a moment.

His face was blank, and it was impossible to tell what the orc might have been thinking.

But at that moment, the fairy Zell tumbled free of its wrapping and zoomed into the air, taking hold of Bash's ear and whispering into it. All of a sudden, Bash's eyebrows shot up.

Then he turned to Houston, his expression composed. Slowly, he nodded.

"Hmm. You may be right there."

"I thought so!"

Houston grinned, pleased that his hunch had proven to be correct.

Houston was a smart man. In the span of a few seconds, he'd already come up with a way to get the orc in his debt, while at the same time preventing any disturbances in town *and* making sure he kept himself out of harm's way.

Houston Jale wasn't exactly a saint, you see.

And he never hesitated to seize any opportunity that might improve his own fortunes later down the line.

"In that case, I'll send young Judith to accompany you. She was the one in charge of the carriage ambush investigation, after all. If you're off investigating it, she's the best person to have assisting you."

"What?"

Judith was standing by the entrance with an extremely displeased look on her face.

"Hold on just a minute, General Houston! You seriously intend to send me off with this wild beast who thinks of nothing else but violating every woman he sees?!"

Judith took an enraged step forward, jabbing an accusatory finger at Bash.

Bash gazed coolly at the finger, responding in a low voice.

"We orcs are forbidden from nonconsensual relations by peace treaty decree. I have no intention of violating you."

Houston looked on, nodding, feeling deeply inspired all of a sudden.

Now that he cast his mind back, he recalled that Bash was never known for dragging women away after battle, even if the entire enemy unit had been wiped out. The other orcs would ignore direct orders and take women right there on the bloody battlefield. But not Bash.

Indeed, it was in an orc's nature to want to ravish as many women as he could.

But this frank, seemingly decent orc clearly intended to hold out against the innate urges of his race and uphold the law of the Orc King.

"See? There, you have the word of the orc himself."

"Seriously?! You of all people should know, General Houston, that orcs are a race of indiscriminate brutes! No matter what he may say, it's obvious that the moment he gets me alone in a dark corner, he'll show his true, despicable colors!"

Houston grabbed Judith by the collar and drew her close until his face was up against hers.

"Shut your mouth, knight. Now listen here. This gentleman is nothing like those rogue orcs. He is the Orc Hero Bash."

"Huh? Hero? Says who?! He's probably just the Orc King's favorite nephew or something!"

Houston was getting a headache.

The Orc Hero Bash was known to every single soldier in the Orc Response Force during the war.

Houston was aware that Judith was a novice knight who'd only joined the service after the war was over. Even so...how could she be so uninformed?!

"..."

Houston fought hard to suppress a sudden urge to scream at the stupid young knight.

The war had been over for three years.

Those who had been soldiers during the war had mostly all returned to their hometowns. To live a peaceful life, away from fighting.

The majority of the soldiers in this town had never even tasted war.

And while most knew of the existence of the Orc King, few knew his name—Nemesis.

What's more, there was still hardly any trading going on between the Fortified City and the orc country. Judith—in fact, all of his subordinates—had only ever encountered rogue orcs. Detestable criminals with no respect for the rules. So Houston supposed her ignorance couldn't be helped.

"He is exalted among orcs, a fact which remains true despite your ignorance. He is an elite, the likes of which a stupid, lowly knight of your ilk could never even hope to converse with."

"What...seriously? But he's just an orc..."

"He has come to Krassel in peace, but make no mistake, if you had truly angered him, you would already be dead."

"Huh...?"

Judith still didn't quite seem to understand.

Houston decided to change tack.

"If you end up sparking another conflict with the orcs, your head will roll. I'll see that you end up executed for it. Do you really want to go to the guillotine during peacetime?"

"The guillo...? But... I mean... He's an *orc*..."

Houston knew he was a coward, an opportunist.

During the war, he had managed to evade Bash, and he carried an odd sense of pride within himself for that *achievement*.

But the others didn't know about all that. Judith and the rest of his subordinates—they all thought Houston was a ruthless, fearsome warrior.

So she was taking his words not as sage advice, but as threats and intimidation.

Judith was still young and inexperienced, and she could not help quaking in her boots.

"Oi."

Bash intervened. There was an angry edge to his voice for the first time, and he was glaring at Houston sharply.

"Unhand the woman."

Houston let go of Judith instantly, hands opening wide as if to say, *I wasn't even touching her, I swear.*

"Is... Is something amiss?"

"You brute..."

Bash paused for a moment, as if weighing his words, before continuing.

"Harassing a woman like that, barking orders at her. Are you not ashamed?"

"I... But..."

Houston's cheeks burned red.

Judith had hauled in Bash, an innocent orc, put him in jail, and interrogated him, all under human jurisdiction. And now she had the nerve to insult Bash right to his face.

Houston could tell what Bash was thinking. Obviously, he was infuriated. But he was trying not to show it. Instead, he was speaking as if in sympathy with Judith's situation.

If it had been any other orc, Houston would have scoffed aloud.

It doesn't matter that she's a woman; she's still my subordinate. It's none of your business, so piss off, he might have said.

Or he might have mocked the orc. *So you got caught, pissed your pants, but then managed to swing the interrogation in your favor, so you decided to get a little too big for your boots, hmm?*

But no, this was no ordinary orc. This was an orc who could disembowel every human in the vicinity before you'd even blinked.

An orc had no need of words. He could demonstrate to the humans just how weak and puny they were through use of his mighty fists.

But Bash hadn't used his fists. Even despite all the humiliation he'd endured.

From where did he get such self-restraint?

Bash was clearly thinking from a loyal orc tribesman's perspective. If Bash attacked any of the humans present, he would be in violation of the wishes of the Orc King. And if Bash turned against the Orc King, many hot-blooded young orcs would follow suit.

That would lead to another war between the orcs and one of the other races. During the long war, the orcs had lost so many of their number. If another war came about, this time, the orc race might go extinct for real.

And so Bash controlled himself.

For the sake of duty, for the future of orckind, Bash could sacrifice his dignity a hundred times over.

For all the power Bash possessed, he refused to use it for his own selfish means, instead devoting himself in service to his race.

What a fine orc he was.

So much more magnanimous, so much more tolerant than could even have been imagined...

Houston felt increasingly ashamed in comparison.

Bash was right. What must the orc have thought of him, haranguing a woman in this way? How pathetic!

As a general—nay, as a man—he could not act like this.

And so Houston made up his mind. A decision that might end up enraging the orc, and yet...he knew what needed to be done.

"You're right, of course. Yes. In that case...I shall accompany you in searching the forest!"

Bash's eye twitched for a moment, but Houston, overwhelmed by the greatness of this mighty orc, failed to notice.

5
TRACKING

Bash was dreaming.

In the dream, he was a young warrior again, still new to the battlefield.

On the day in the dream, Bash and his company were hiding in the undergrowth, preparing to launch a surprise attack on the enemy.

"Listen, fellas... If you were gonna take a wife, what would ya want 'er to be like?"

As they hunkered down in the thick undergrowth, it was the orc Bulfitt who posed that question.

Bulfitt had a deep wound on his neck—a souvenir from the previous battle. The attack he'd suffered should have beheaded him, but thanks to his tough orc hide, he'd not only kept his head, but his carotid artery wasn't even nicked.

Even the toughest-skinned orcs sometimes need medical care to avoid the grave.

But Bulfitt had battled on, almost unaware of his injury. His counterattack took down his assailant, and he was able to withdraw without further incident.

Bulfitt had already told that particular war story a hundred times.

He was truly a heroic orc.

"I think, for me, I'd want a strong woman."

Biggden was one of the bulkiest orcs in their company.

Orcs often threw themselves fully into battle. In the thick of war, strength and sheer size were almost equal in terms of battle advantage. The bigger you were, the easier it was to ignore superficial wounds and keep fighting. And of course, you would be able to carry much heftier weapons.

The sight of Biggden flailing two gigantic clubs in the air would be enough to make any orc hold their breath in admiration.

Despite fighting in countless battles, Biggden bore no major scars. Of all Bash's company, he was perhaps the most promising future star.

"I like a woman who knows 'er own mind. And if it's humans we're talkin' about, I'd like a lady knight. A strong warrior for me missus, now that'd be just fine with me."

Donzoi was missing the ring finger and pinky finger of his left hand, and his entire body was disfigured with burns.

He had been set on fire by a mage in his first-ever battle.

If there hadn't been a pond located conveniently nearby, Donzoi would have burned to death.

Ever since then, Donzoi always carried a waterskin inside his armor. He was the best-prepared orc of Bash's generation. Donzoi would study the enemy, identify any weaknesses, and think of the best way to approach them. He put great care into choosing his shield or making his own fire bottles and other inventive weapons and tools to bring to the battlefield. Many an army general had been saved by Donzoi's ingenuity.

"I know what ya mean. A warrior, eh? She'd put up a good fight. Unbreakable spirit, ya know? That wouldn't fade, not even after already whelpin' three young'uns for ya. Imagine 'avin' yer way with 'er in front of all 'er troops... Makes me hard just thinkin' about it!"

Budarth was a red orc with a huge cross-shaped scar across his entire face. He was Bash's platoon captain.

His meaty arms were twice the circumference of any other orc's, and he had the strength to match his size.

He had been born from a dwarf woman and had nimble fingers. He was an archer who fought with a sort of hybrid bow. The bow was designed to work with an orc's mighty arm strength, and it was a formidable weapon indeed. With it, Budarth was capable of pinning a horse to a tree or shooting a wyvern clean out of the sky.

As the platoon captain, he had a good head on his shoulders, but he was also arrogant and somewhat stuck-up. Just because he was one of the rarer red orc variety, that made him think he was better than the others.

"If we want to get wives someday, we need to prove ourselves..."

Bash was the best swordsman in the group. But at that time, he still hadn't made a name for himself. He was the smallest orc in the platoon, and his skin was just an ordinary green color.

Bash wasn't a nobody, far from it. He just hadn't begun to stand out yet.

"Hmm. They're close."

"Time to boogie, fellas."

"All right, 'ere they come. Quiet down, all of ya!"

They all fell silent, complying with Budarth's command.

Moments later, the sound of horses' hooves could be heard. It seemed like the enemy party was trying to be as quiet as possible, but the orcs' keen ears picked up on every little sound.

Bash's group waited until they could hear the horses breathing, and then...

"GRAGH!"

They pounced.

The enemy party consisted of about five knights and another thirty foot soldiers. A mid-sized platoon.

The orc company, however, numbered only five. The enemy had the advantage, but Bash's company did not know the meaning of the word *retreat*. Instead, they launched a furious attack.

...Biggden died in that battle.

When Bash awoke, he found himself lying down in an unfamiliar room.

Where am I?

As Bash sat up in bed, the events of the previous day came flooding back to him.

Things had ended up with him being paired with Judith, and they were to go out and investigate the forest road ambush together.

It had been too late the previous day, though—the sun was already setting on the horizon. So Bash was shown to a private chamber in the fortress and invited to spend the night.

So I'm in Krassel, huh?

Bash sighed, pondering the dream he'd been having.

Yes... We often used to have talks like that...

Meeting Judith yesterday must have caused him to dream that particular dream.

Judith...the woman who had appeared in his life so suddenly. She was a beauty, and perhaps as a result of daily, vigorous sword training, she had one hell of a hot body. Her voice was pleasant to the ear, as well. Bash wished he could have listened to her talk more.

To add to all that, she was a knight—every orc's dream woman.

A knight would be prideful and wouldn't give up, right to the bitter end. Forcefully impregnating a haughty woman who fought back the entire time...that was every orc's most erotic fantasy.

Bash's circle of orcs were all in agreement that a knight or a princess was the best option for a wife.

Personally, Bash didn't care whether a woman was a princess or a knight or what have you. Any woman would do when it came to shedding his virginity.

But Judith... Judith was the embodiment of every red-blooded orc's deepest desires. As Bash pictured losing his virginity with Judith, the blood all rushed to a certain part of his body, instantly engorging it.

What a lucky orc I am to have met a gorgeous lady knight like her so soon into my search.

"Ah, mornin', Boss."

While Bash sat there, enraptured by his own fantasies, Zell stopped grooming their fairy wings and turned to him with a big grin.

"You're very, um, *perky* this morning. Thinking about paying that lady knight a visit, are ya?"

"Something like that."

"You know, Boss, this is the first time I've seen you in all your *morning glory*. It's just as magnificent as I'd imagined."

"Is it?"

Bash felt his chest swell with pride.

Orcs felt no embarrassment when others noticed they'd pitched a tent in their pants. In fact, an orc's erection was a symbol of his virility and manhood, and the general consensus was that it was something worth showing off. Being complimented on the size of their member was an orc's second-favorite thing to hear.

The thing they liked to hear best of all, of course, was praise for their physical strength.

"That knight, Judith, I bet she's a virgin for sure! She'll probably squeal like a piglet when you stick it to her!"

Zell was trying to sound casual and boorish, but actually, the fairy seemed a bit embarrassed by their own words.

Yes, Zell was facing Bash, grinning widely, but their eyes were darting this way and that.

"But are you sure she's the woman you want?"

"What do you mean?"

"I just think... Y'know, she was awfully impudent considering she's just a rookie knight. She arrested you and looked down on you. I'm a broad-minded fairy, but even I was starting to get pissed off."

"I don't mind that. I like a woman with fire."

"You like strong-willed women, Boss?"

"Of course. All orcs do."

Having said that, the previous day's encounter with Judith was the first time Bash had ever met a strong-willed woman, let alone spoken to one.

All of the female soldiers he'd met in the past he'd just attacked on sight.

Incidentally, this supposed orc penchant for strong-willed women... Bash had only ever heard this from lecherous orcs during bawdy conversations. But he'd heard it so often that he had internalized it, and now he, too, believed that feisty women were best.

"Hmm, I see, I see...," muttered Zell under their breath.

Then they began gathering up the fairy dust they'd dropped and putting it neatly into a tiny glass bottle.

Fairy dust had unusual power. When sprinkled on a wound, it would instantly soothe and heal. When swallowed, it would recover energy and strength. Taken regularly, it could cure most illnesses, and it even had beautifying properties.

It was something of a panacea.

It was one of a fairy's main functions, but it was also the reason humans, with their weak bodies, sought to capture them. The fairies were aware that many different races were keen to get their hands on their dust, and so they began proactively export-ing it for sale.

Since fairies have tiny bodies, they can only make a little fairy dust at a time. Fairy dust also rapidly loses potency. Thus, unsatisfied by the concept of fair trade, the humans still sought to poach fairies for captivity.

"Here, Boss."

"...May I?"

"Sure! Consider it thanks for saving me! Oh, but one request...could you use it somewhere I can't see you? Thanks."

Zell offered the tiny bottle to Bash, blushing.

Fairies generally hated giving away their fairy dust.

They regard their dust as waste, no different from feces. No matter how ephem-eral fairies may be, having to watch other people smearing their "excrement" on their wounds or swallowing it...grosses them out.

Actually, the fairies who stayed behind in their own country during the war never even knew what uses their fairy dust was being put to.

How the fairies laughed to learn that humans raised crops using their *own crap* as fertilizer. *Ew, gross!*

But Zell was one of the fairies who had survived the war.

It was still embarrassing, of course, but Zell had mostly managed to push through it.

"Thank you."

Nodding, Bash gratefully accepted the bottle.

"This will come in handy. I don't know how many times I've relied on this stuff before now."

Back when he was still a rookie, Bash had suffered a serious injury, but fairy dust had saved his life.

By the time the war was reaching its final stages, Bash had made it through with no further serious injuries. He'd used fairy dust regularly just to keep himself going so he could battle for days on end.

He probably wouldn't need any fairy dust on this journey, though.

Still, Bash was grateful. Having a bottle on hand would be very reassuring.

"All right, you should get dressed, and then..."

Suddenly, Zell trailed off mid-sentence.

"Wake up, orc! General Houston said to show you to..."

The door had been flung open all of a sudden, and Judith's face appeared, peeking around the doorframe.

She was staring at Bash, who was standing there stark naked and well-muscled from head to toe, his orc pride rising tall from his groin for all to see.

"..."

Judith instantly went white and appeared to stop breathing.

Bash knew the look in her eyes.

Rage.

Judith was so upset, she couldn't even speak. But Bash had no idea why.

The previous night, Bash had removed his armor since he would be sleeping indoors and had gone to bed naked. Surely, that couldn't be what Judith was angry about, could it?

"What is it?"

"Just...get ready. I'll be, um, waiting...outside..."

"All right."

If Bash had done something to offend the lady, then he was indeed sorry. But he was also an orc. An orc never apologized without at least knowing what he did wrong.

"What could have angered her...?"

"She's had a stick up her butt since yesterday. Maybe angry is just her default mood?"

"No, today she seemed completely different than she did yesterday."

"Eh, I guess."

There was definitely something up with Judith. But Bash wasn't socially aware enough to identify or articulate what that was. Nor did he know much about humans to begin with.

"At any rate, you better not keep her waiting! Hurry and get ready! Then go get that lady knight in the sack!"

"I will!"

Once they were ready to go, the two of them left the room together.

The western forest region of Krassel...

A single highway ran through the forest. It had been constructed for transportation during the war. It was named the Brikuus Highway after the general who'd commissioned its construction. In the western part of the forest, the highway split into two roads. One led to the country of the elves, the other to the country of the orcs.

Despite being called a highway, it was more of a narrow dirt track that could barely fit a single horse-drawn carriage.

The orc country didn't get that many visitors, and if one wanted to go to elf country, there were other, safer roads to take. So traffic was rare along the highway.

Incidentally, the reason Bash hadn't taken this highway was because orcs generally stayed off the roads, as a rule.

An orc would never lose his way in the forest, and a little rough terrain was nothing to them. So really, they had no need of roads.

Recently, an incident had occurred on the Brikuus Highway.

A horse-drawn wagon had been ambushed by bugbears, and the merchants riding on the wagon had been killed.

Actually, this kind of thing happened a lot.

Even though the war was over, that didn't mean there were any fewer wild beasts that preyed on humans around.

These unintelligent creatures roamed the forest freely, attacking people every now and again.

Actually, it was more than every now and again. It was all the time lately.

So the general, Houston, had tasked the hunters with locating and suppressing the bugbears in particular.

When the wild beast population grew out of control, regular attacks like these were the result.

A cull was the only logical recourse.

The hunters had already wiped out several bugbear packs.

Eliminating every single one in the western forest wasn't feasible, but taking out some of the larger packs should have proven quite effective.

After that, the issue ought to have been resolved for a time.

The attacks didn't stop completely, but the humans were confident the frequency of them would decline considerably.

That didn't happen, though.

The attacks continued with the exact same frequency of occurrence, even after the bugbear cull.

Something was strange. Suspicious, Houston put the rookie knight Judith in charge of the investigation.

Judith may have been a rookie, but she'd been a knight for a whole year now. It was high time she took on some more responsibility.

Judith embarked on the investigation with relish. A promising young knight, she was nervous to be tackling her first important mission. Nonetheless, she managed to gather several intriguing pieces of information. First, she confirmed that the western forest region was only very sparsely inhabited by bugbears to begin with.

And with the recent culls—if the hunters' reports were correct, that is—there should have been even fewer.

She also discovered that several loads of cargo being transported by the merchants had gone missing. Not so many as to be immediately obvious without checking the stock lists of major trading companies, but there were definitely important items missing.

Bugbears and other wild beasts might drag away interesting cargo on occasion, but on a scale this big...? Unlikely.

From those two pieces of information, Houston surmised that these attacks were being committed not by wild animals but by people.

Whoever was behind it all was making it *look* like bugbear attacks and then pilfering subtle amounts of the goods from the wagons.

To date, the humans hadn't managed to apprehend the criminal responsible.

Attacks kept happening. But all that was left behind afterward were bugbear tracks.

The bugbears knew to stay away when guards were sent accompanying the merchant wagons. But in recent years, inexperienced and enthusiastic sellers had increased in number, and few of them paid any heed to the dangers of traveling without protection.

Eyewitness reports from survivors mentioned bugbears on the scene, but none recalled seeing anyone else.

Aware of the preciousness of human lives, Houston felt he could not, in good conscience, post spies in the forest to potentially witness an attack from start to finish.

And so Judith's investigation had reached a standstill.

She had no new leads, no clues, and no suspects. All she had were more questions. Judith started to become increasingly stressed-out.

This was her first real mission, and she was failing miserably.

Just as Judith was nearing her wit's end, another attack occurred.

She and her troops had been patrolling the forest when they stumbled across a horse-drawn carriage that had only just been attacked.

As always, there were no potential suspects in sight.

But on closer inspection of the scene, they located orc footprints. The prints led them all the way back to Krassel. Then, while gathering reports in the town, they discovered that an orc had been seen recently passing through the gates. They also received a report from two traumatized female merchants, claiming they had been attacked by an orc in the forest.

Judith had leaped on this new information and quickly continued the investigation.

She found out that the orc the women had been attacked by was staying at an inn in town.

Further investigation would have made it clear that this orc had not been the instigator of the carriage ambush. But by this time, Judith was too frenzied to think clearly.

Instead, she was extremely excited. Finally, she had a clue. Breathing hard, she spoke to her men. *"This is unbelievable! The culprits were right here in town, right under our noses, and we didn't realize it! That's it! We're going to round up every last potential thief in town, starting with the orc!!!"*

Then Judith had instructed her men to surround the inn, and after that, Bash had been arrested on a case of mistaken identity.

"So this is the scene. What do you make of it, Mr. Bash?"

Bash had been brought back to the scene of the ambush. The broken carriage was still lying on its side. As was the several-day-old horse corpse, which was abuzz with flies.

There were also tracks. Obvious ones.

There were three different types of tracks in all: the merchant women's tracks, Bash's tracks, and countless bugbear tracks.

"It looks like it was a straightforward bugbear ambush to me."

After looking around the scene, that was the only hypothesis Bash could think of.

Bash had seen ambushes like this during the war, often caused by the enemy troops, but sometimes by wild beasts and monsters. Orc warriors may have been plentiful, but if they ever ended up outnumbered in a wild beast ambush, their survival would not have been guaranteed.

The scene in front of him now looked like the aftermath of a standard ambush attack.

"Hmph, so you're just a regular orc after all. Taking it at face value, are you?"

"Hmm..."

Judith mockingly snorted at Bash. Bash was a warrior and wasn't accustomed to these types of investigations. All he could do was describe the scene as he saw it. But he wished he could say something—anything—that would impress Judith.

"Well...first off, there are no other footprints besides those of the merchant women. The cargo, too, appears mostly untouched. If an enemy force had waylaid the carriage, there is no way they would have left the spoils behind. Particularly food and water. Those would have been the first things they took. If this was wartime, it would be easy to chalk this up to nothing more than a random bugbear attack."

"Right. Go on..."

Bash thought hard, his small brain working as fast as it could go.

He hadn't used his brain like this in a long while, not since that time the dwarf troops almost had him buried alive in the Aryoshiya Caves.

Bash had used all the local environmental information available to him on that scene in order to escape.

"If this is the work of sentient beings, then there has to be some sort of objective behind it."

"That's what we've been *saying*. Their objective is to attack the merchants but avoid suspicion by making it look like random wild animal attacks. Because if the blame falls on animals, they won't be suspected, and they can continue stealing to their hearts' content. Honestly, orcs are so stupid. You're nothing but dead weight to this investigation..."

"Hmm..."

Bash glanced at his partner, the fairy.

In situations like this, orcs often turned to their fairy companions, the scouts, for their opinions.

Zell zoomed around the scene, doing tumbling somersaults in the air as they thought hard. Then, drawing level with Bash's eyeline, they shook their head.

"Well, judging by the scene, a bugbear attack is the only explanation I can think of as well."

"Oh, is it, now?! See, you're useless. This is a complex issue. We've been investigating it for ages and still don't know who's behind it. It's not like it's something super obvious, something you two jerks could figure out from just a glance at the scene, you know."

Judith puffed up her chest haughtily as she said this, even though her team's failure was nothing to brag about.

But Zell had no idea, either, nor did Bash.

"Shall we get on with the tracking, then?"

"Yes, let's head to the next area."

"Next area? What are you talking about?"

Still puffed up with indignance, Judith narrowed her eyes at the fairy and the orc.

"Why, tracking the bugbears, of course."

Zell shrugged, but Judith's frown only deepened.

"Tracking? Don't be absurd. Bugbears are incredibly cunning. Even our best hunters can't track them."

As a rule, bugbears didn't leave *tracks*.

At least, that was the general human consensus. Bugbears were adept at hiding their own tracks and were even careful not to poop anywhere but safe within their own lairs.

To get back to their lairs without leaving evidence, bugbears would cross rivers and even climb through trees. Anything to avoid leaving prints.

In order to draw out and capture a bugbear, the hunters had to burn special incense to entice them.

This incense was made from bugbear blood. The scent of this burning incense would confuse bugbears into thinking their territory was under attack, and the whole pack would come running to fight.

As long as the incense was burned in areas that actually contained bugbears, that is.

"Really? Humans can't track them?"

These beliefs about bugbears never leaving tracks were generally held only by the human race.

Other races knew better.

"Are you saying fairies can?!"

"No, no, fairies don't partake in tracking or other such animalistic practices. And besides, we have no reason to go pursuing bugbears. They don't even exist in fairy country, so nobody cares. Certainly, no one would care to go tracking them..."

Actually, bugbears didn't traditionally dwell in human country, either.

After the war, they began to appear within the human borders.

Why was this so? Had the bugbears relocated? Unlikely. Bugbears were highly territorial wild beasts. No, they would never leave their original homes.

Actually, there was a logical explanation. It was because the humans had seized land that used to belong to another race. And they had discovered bugbears dwelling on this land. Perhaps it had always originally been bugbear territory.

"If you wanna track a bugbear, you've gotta ask the orcs. They've been doing it for hundreds of years!"

Right, this land was originally part of the orc country.

Wild beasts were vermin.

Left unculled, they would infiltrate the towns and villages, destroy crops, and attack livestock.

When their numbers were plentiful, they would even attack people.

There were not so many differences between ordinary wild beasts and demonic beasts. One key difference was that demonic beasts tended to appear from out of the ether, apparently not from natural reproductive means.

Although some said the key difference was that only demonic beasts attacked humans unprovoked.

Actually, the beastkin, demons, and orcs—races now classed as sentient beings—were considered equivalent to mythical creatures and monsters pre-war. The human historical records even described them as such.

The bugbears were viewed by orcs as a type of mythical creature, too, but were treated much the same as other wild animals.

They weren't very tasty, but their large size and the sheer number of them meant that they made suitable food for the orcs.

As a result, orcs became skilled at hunting the bugbears. Orc hunters would get up with the dawn and head out to track them. The early bird gets the worm, after all.

During the war, Bash himself had often hunted bugbears.

"..."

Bash was silent now, solemnly following the bugbears' trail.

He hadn't been hunting in a while, but it still came easy to him.

Bugbears may have been crafty, but even they weren't able to hide their tracks completely.

The saliva they tended to drop as they moved between trees actually had a distinctive smell and was a huge clue.

Orcs had keen noses. Their sense of smell was particularly attuned to the distinct odors of wild beasts. They could pick up on scents human hunters would barely even notice. In fact, the orcs were said to have a sense of smell that was even keener than that of the beastkin race.

To put it another way, there was no hope of tracking a bugbear without an orc's nose to guide the way.

Bugbears were almost pathologically obsessed with hiding their own tracks. If you did happen to catch sight of a bugbear print, it was likely to be extremely faint, or even only partially formed, so much so that you would doubt your own eyes. Bugbears would also sometimes intentionally leave fake prints that led in the opposite direction of their lairs, just to throw off would-be pursuers.

"I heard that orcs have a keen nose for tracking down wild beasts, but I had no idea..."

Houston was gazing with awe at Bash, who was busy tracking. His voice was filled with wonder.

"It's not so impressive. You know as well as anyone that our noses are easier to fool than, say, a beastkin's."

"Ah... Well..."

Bash's pointed response made Houston smile weakly.

Yes, orcs may have been blessed with keen noses, but not discerning ones. For an orc was unable to categorize different smells. In the past, the humans had exploited this weakness by luring the orcs to one place and then ambushing the entire group of them.

Houston found his thoughts returning to the war.

He had once lured Bash into a trap using just such a technique in the hopes of killing him.

"At any rate, this tracking method should bring us right to the bugbears that were responsible for the ambush."

Bash was leading the group, which also consisted of seven humans.

There were Houston and Judith, plus five foot soldiers. The soldiers had all been trained by Houston himself.

The five of them had served faithfully under Houston since back during the war... Of course, they all knew about Bash. But they were only foot soldiers. None of them had any particular interest in getting to know the enemy, and none were experts on orcs, as Houston was.

The full weight of the title Orc Hero didn't really register with them.

All they knew was that there had been a particularly wild orc warrior on the battlefield during the war.

Before setting out, Houston had gathered his soldiers around him. "*He may be an orc, but he's an orc of significant status. You don't need to be on your guard around him.*" Or so he had told them. But the foot soldiers continued to view Bash as an unknown and potentially threatening entity.

The soldiers remained on high alert around Bash, making sure to stay aware of their surroundings so that they could react quickly if the orc launched a surprise attack.

In fact, they were somewhat confused. Why was General Houston expressing such goodwill toward an orc? It was extremely strange.

"Has the general lost his mind? And he's usually so ruthless toward the orcs, too..."

"No idea."

"Hmm, maybe something happened with this particular orc during the war."

The soldiers muttered among themselves, trying to make sense of Houston's strange attitude.

"Yeah, it doesn't track. Maybe this orc has placed some sort of magic charm on him?"

"Yeah, maybe. Anyway, if Houston the Pig Slayer is willing to vouch for him, then he must be a special sort of orc."

"Right, there are some good folks to be found out there, even among the harpies and the lizardmen. It stands to reason there has to be at least a few half-decent orcs."

"You're probably right. This orc does seem pretty unusual."

Through this hushed discussion, the soldiers managed to come to a general consensus on Bash's supposed credentials, although one person remained unconvinced.

That person, of course, was Judith.

"...Hmph."

As the other soldiers began to increasingly warm toward Bash, only Judith remained ice-cold, fixing the orc with a hateful glare.

"...!"

All of a sudden, Bash turned around.

Judith looked away in a panic. Then she realized that she had no reason to feel flustered and trained her gaze on him again, in a challenging manner.

Bash simply gazed back at Judith's scowl with a neutral expression on his face.

For a few moments, they contemplated each other. Judith narrowed her eyes, daring Bash to be the first to look away. If she showed the slightest hint of weakness now, the orc would soon start throwing his weight about and trying to intimidate her. She just knew it.

"Huh."

As if reading Judith's mind, the orc rolled his eyes a little, eventually looking away.

"Hey!"

Judith knew what that look meant.

The orc was mocking her. It was as if he was saying she was too insignificant to even bother with.

How dare this orc look down on me!

Of course, Bash had no such intentions.

He was merely putting into practice what he'd learned from the lesson on human women Zell had given him. **Rule Number Four: Give Her an Appreciative Glance** and **Rule Number Five: Give Her a Suggestive Smile**.

Apparently, human women loved what Zell called "the male gaze." They also apparently liked men who were *mysterious*.

Zell had assured Bash that any woman would go weak in the knees for a man who could whip out a suggestive smile at the critical moment.

Going weak in the knees over a smile... Could human women really be that easy?

At any rate, Bash's attempts didn't seem to be having the desired effect on Judith.

"Is something amiss, Mr. Bash?"

"No, nothing... Incidentally, we are getting close now."

Houston clamped his lips tightly together and raised one hand in the air.

At his signal, the foot soldiers all came to a sudden halt. With a final *clank* of their armor, they froze completely still.

Despite being clad in heavy armor, Houston's soldiers were able to stand stock-still, making not even the slightest *clink* or *clank*. These soldiers had survived on the battlefield, where making the slightest noise could often mean death.

"Judith, it is time for the silencing."

"Yes, sir."

Judith withdrew her wand from her belt at Houston's command, her face solemn and serious.

Then, muttering an incantation under her breath, Judith began to cast silencing magic on each soldier in turn.

This type of support magic required the caster to touch the recipient's body.

Naturally, Judith paused before touching Bash. But, aware of her superior's eyes on her, she knew she could not shy away from him. This was still her first mission, and she'd proven herself completely useless so far. She certainly wasn't about to hinder things further by letting her own sense of disgust get in the way.

With a look of revulsion on her face, Judith placed her hand on Bash's bulky shoulder.

"Unf!"

Just then, Bash let out a strange grunt.

Judith shrank back, startled.

"What? What is it?"

"Ah... I apologize. It is just that your hand is so...cold."

Bash somehow managed to cover for himself. In truth, he had been shaken by the unexpectedly soft touch of a woman's hand, a touch he had never felt before now. He was suddenly overcome with a huge urge to throw Judith to the ground and make babies with her right then and there, in front of everyone.

But he restrained himself.

He no longer needed Zell's help to guess that a human woman would not take kindly to such a thing.

Especially not a strong-willed woman like Judith.

During the war, Bash had once seen a great chief carrying a woman like a sack of potatoes. She was screaming and carrying on and seemed quite upset, all because the great chief had clearly just finished having his way with her.

The great chief had actually been quite playful with the woman, toying with her during the mating act. It had not appeared violent, as was the usual way. The spectating orcs nearby had all been smiling and chuckling while watching. But the woman had seemed frantic. Apparently, such a thing was a bigger deal to humans.

If an orc was to do such a thing in this postwar era, perhaps it would be considered nonconsensual.

And so Bash girded his loins and tried desperately to slow his rapid breathing.

Rule Number 6: *He Who Loudly Pants Will Never Get Into Her Pants.*

When orcs were confronted with either a battle or a woman, they had a tendency to pant and snort loudly. But human women apparently did not care for this, considering it barbarous behavior.

As Bash held himself together, his body began to sparkle slightly. It was a sign that the spell had taken hold.

"All right. First off, let's send a scout ahead."

The moment Houston suggested it, Zell shot forward.

"A scout, you say? Leave it to me! I'm ready to dive into the thick of danger. I'd even fly right into the fires of Mount Bafar itself!"

Then, without bothering to wait for a response, Zell zoomed off deep into the forest without a backward glance. "I'll be back before sundown!" the fairy yelped before disappearing among the trees.

"Hmm, well, I see no harm in leaving it to Scout Zell."

Houston knew quite a bit about Zell, too.

That fairy could sniff out the enemy's position no matter how well they were hiding.

Zell would infiltrate the enemy HQ itself and guide Bash's company right to the spot. Then carnage would ensue. Yes, Zell was an expert scout and spy. Houston knew all about Zell.

"Hmm... Yes, I suppose..."

"Anyway, let's hold our position here until Scout Zell returns."

"Mm-hmm."

Bash nodded, but his brow was furrowed.

Bash knew Zell would locate the enemy—that much was certain. The only problem was half the time when Zell found the enemy, the enemy also found Zell...

And just as Bash had feared, Zell did not return.

6
Fake-Bait Zell

With their small stature and ability to fly at top speeds, the fairy race should have been ideally suited for performing reconnaissance.

The truth, however, was very different. All fairies emitted a faint glow. In the darkness of night or the deep forest, this light made them immediately conspicuous. Still, considering the tiny size and sheer speed of fairies, this glow shouldn't have been such a serious handicap.

The problem wasn't the glow, per se. It was the fairy tendency to completely forget about this characteristic of theirs.

Fairies often hid their heads while neglecting to hide their butts, so to speak.

A fairy hiding in the darkness, completely unaware of its own glow... Such a fairy was bound to be captured.

Luckily, fairies were rarely ever killed after capture. They were valued for their medicinal properties, of course. But many folks were also superstitious when it came to fairies, believing that anyone who murdered a fairy would be doomed to the fires of hell.

At any rate, Bash wasn't expecting much from Zell's scouting effort on this occasion.

As long as Zell made it back alive, that was fine with him. Even Zell wouldn't be so careless as to get captured by bugbears. And if Zell ran afoul of humans, there was no need to worry about them killing the little scout. Besides, even if Zell did get captured, Bash would simply follow the fairy's scent, as he had during the war days.

But as Bash had predicted, the fairy did not return.

"It seems the fairy has indeed been captured."

Bash and company followed Zell's scent, and it led them to a strange place.

The gaping maw of a cave peeked from the rocks in front of them. The opening was actually ingeniously covered with creeping ivy vines. Houston and the other humans had completely failed to notice the hidden cave at first.

"This is the work of sentient beings. Someone must be controlling the bugbears, using them for their own devices."

"Beast tamers, you mean?"

Members of the demon race were long known for capturing and training wild animals and monsters to do their bidding. During the war, their training techniques were utilized only by the Coalition of Seven Races, but over many years of battle, the practice came to be well-studied and was eventually adopted by every country.

One particularly popular anecdote about beast taming involved the humans and their successful manipulation of a large dragon.

After the war, each country cut their army down to size dramatically, and many ex-soldiers found themselves with no vocation in life.

Many former beast tamers ended up turning their hand to theft and burglary.

"In that case, we need to infiltrate and ambush them! We can extract the fairy and kill all the beast tamers and bugbears at the same time! Right, General Houston?"

Judith sounded excited by the prospect of action. If the fairy had been captured, well then, they would simply rescue it. That was the obvious course of action.

"No... We should wait until nightfall."

Houston did not share Judith's opinion.

"We don't know the ins and outs of this cave, nor do we know how many of the enemy to expect. I won't risk our safety. We will wait until nightfall."

"But, sir!"

This was a cave, possibly the main hideout of the enemy. The usual procedure in this kind of situation would be to return to town and get backup. Then, with twenty or thirty soldiers from the town, they would surround the area and smoke out the enemy without ever needing to set foot inside themselves.

Usually, that was precisely what Houston would do.

But right now, one of their own was captured.

And they had no way of knowing how the criminals might be treating their captive.

After conducting their operation in such secrecy so far, the enemy might think to kill the fairy upon realizing they had been cornered.

Still, Zell probably wouldn't be killed right away.

Zell was only a fairy and had come alone. As long as the tiny creature didn't run their mouth, the criminals had no reason to believe they'd been tracked.

Besides, Zell had survived of countless wartime battles. Surely, they wouldn't let vital information slip.

Zell had probably already been bottled up for use as a portable medicine source.

If Houston were in the enemy's boots, however, he would not bottle Zell. He would consider a fairy wandering into their cave as a bad omen and would kill them immediately. Then he would evacuate at once.

But the criminals had been doing very well for themselves so far. It didn't seem likely that they would throw their whole operation down the drain just because of a small fly in the ointment. So the fairy was most likely safe.

Still, Houston was not blind to the possible complications afoot.

If Zell flapped those fairy gums and said too much...

My buddies are gonna be here any minute to rescue me! They're members of Krassel's self-defense army, you know! You're all gonna get arrested and taken straight to the chopping block!

If the fairy said something like that, then it would all be over.

At first, the criminals would probably laugh, seeing Zell as nothing but a jabbering creature of little significance, fit only for harvesting fairy dust.

At least, until the following day's dawn broke.

Folks have a weird tendency to find sudden clarity the morning after, their brains sorting through information as they sleep and leading them to logical conclusions. When morning came, Zell would be snuffed out, and the criminals would flee. These were sophisticated criminals, after all, who had managed to evade the Krassel investigators while committing serious attacks. Their next move seemed obvious.

To be honest about it, that would be fine with Houston. Then the highway attacks would stop, and Krassel would know peace once more.

The only problem was...Houston's subordinates.

Zell wasn't really Houston's responsibility, but if Houston made the call to abandon a comrade in front of his loyal soldiers... Well, the prospect was simply unthinkable.

And there was Bash to consider, as well. Houston didn't have the guts to condemn this great orc's good friend to death right in front of him.

So he had no choice. He would have to launch a rescue mission using the manpower he currently had at his disposal.

Still, it wouldn't do to risk his soldiers' lives without careful consideration. So to increase their chances of victory, Houston decided on a night raid.

If Zell had run his mouth, then the enemy would be on edge, for sure.

They would be on the alert, ready for an attack at any time. But staying on the alert for a long period of time—that was a difficult thing indeed. If they waited just a little, then the enemy would begin to relax and even fall asleep. Assuming Zell was still alive, this would give them the best chance of rescue.

"Mr. Bash, is that all right with you?"

Houston made sure to double-check his plans with Bash, just in case.

Left to his own devices, the orc would probably barge in by himself and wipe out the entire net of criminals with his own two hands.

In which case, Houston and his men wouldn't even need to go into the cave at all.

If so, *Go ahead, Bash. Be our guest.* But Houston was a careful man.

He knew better than to bet on a wild card.

Of course, if Bash opposed Houston's plan and announced that he was going in alone, then Houston would make no move to stop him.

"...Fine."

But after a few moments of silence, Bash merely agreed with Houston.

Judith was outraged.

"The heck?! You're going to just wait it out, too? That's your buddy they've captured, you know! I thought orcs were supposed to be brave warriors, charging into battle no matter the disadvantages?!"

"Orcs always follow orders first, then we fight bravely doing just as we've been directed. The commanding officer has decided on our plan. I will follow it through as instructed."

The wild, reckless attacks the orcs were still known for had actually only happened during the early stages of the war.

Over time, they had learned many tricks of warfare. Laying an ambush. Attacking by surprise. Taking out enemies troop by troop. Singling out leaders for assassination. Burning the enemy's food supplies. Cutting off their access to fresh water. And so on.

All of these actions involved abiding by a commander's order.

Ironically, it was the human example that had taught the orcs all of this, over the course of about a century.

Even to the present day, orcs were still not capable of the kind of sophistication the humans possessed so naturally. But they had learned to think carefully before they acted.

Had they not, they would never have established their own chain of command, which went from chief to war chief to great chief.

Orcs had also learned to follow the orders of the local clan chief whenever they stayed in the villages of different orc clans.

In other words, Bash being a modern orc and all, he fully intended to comply with whatever orders General Houston came out with.

"Besides, Zell will be just fine."

"You don't have any proof of that. You just...no, forget it! There's no point even talking to you! General Houston, sir. Please give the order. I will lead the other soldiers into the cave and launch an all-out attack, not resting until every criminal has been exterminated!"

Houston scratched his chin as both Bash and Judith looked at him expectantly.

"Hmm. Judith is right. Zell's safety is a serious concern. They say that fairies don't often get killed, but there's no guarantee, is there? So what's your reason for being so confident Zell will be all right?"

"If Zell was weak enough to be killed here, then they would have already died long ago in the war."

Bash's response was brief, but it resonated with Houston. After all, sometimes especially weak or foolish fairies did get killed.

But Zell had survived countless captures during the war and lived to tell the tale.

Perhaps the fairy was simply lucky.

But Houston didn't think so.

Houston had heard tales of the fairy Zell evading capture countless times. No doubt there were many other occasions, too—those that Houston simply hadn't heard about.

If he factored in those unknown incidences as well, then the fairy must have been almost constantly escaping capture. A normal sort of fairy would have been killed a hundred times over in similar circumstances. But Zell had survived. It couldn't simply be chalked up to dumb luck.

"I see. That makes sense. They do call them Fake-Bait Zell. I am not confident, but I am willing to wait and see."

Zell's name was quite famous.

Acquiring a nickname of any kind from the war was a sort of proof that one had managed to distinguish oneself, no matter the actual truth of their deeds.

"All right, everyone. So we wait. We will observe the cave from within the bounds of our silencing spell, and then we will launch an attack on the enemy while they sleep."

Yes, they would wait. That was what Houston decided.

Judith still wasn't convinced.

"But, sir! Please reconsider!"

"What did you say?"

"Our comrade could be in dire straits at this very moment!"

"Indeed. That's possible. I would like to do our best for the little creature, but we have no time to return to the town for reinforcements. So we will launch a midnight attack with the manpower we've got."

"No, we should attack now!"

"I have already spoken on the matter. It is too dangerous right now. We wait."

Houston's tone had grown harsh. Judith clenched her fists and backed down.

And yet she was still frowning with dissension.

The rookie was clearly struggling to respect authority and had been angered by Houston's decision to place more importance on Bash's opinion than hers. She seemed desperate to have things go her way, rather than deferring to Houston as protocol dictated.

Well, I can sympathize. This is her very first mission, after all.

Yes, Houston understood. But right now, he had command of this mission.

The moment Houston had announced he would join the forest search party, this mission ceased to be Judith's.

It was an unsophisticated transfer of power, to be sure. But as long as Houston was in charge, he would do his best to make sure that all of his subordinates made it back alive and that the case was neatly solved.

Yes, that was what Houston planned.

"All right, we'll post one man on lookout duty while the rest get some sleep. Mr. Bash, is that all right with you?"

"I will defer to the commander's order."

Then Bash went right over to a nearby tree, leaned his back up against it, and closed his eyes.

"All right. Jett, you have the first watch. If anything happens, wake us up."

The first lookout went to stand by the cave entrance, on the alert.

Houston guessed they had around five hours to wait before the enemy decided to hit the sack.

When that time came, Houston would let the first lookout sleep while another soldier stood guard over the cave entrance. Those two would be left behind to guard the rear as the others infiltrated the cave.

Houston had two good reasons for leaving a few men behind. First, this would prevent any additional enemies sneaking into the cave in the dead of night and coming up behind them. Second, in the case that Houston's entire party was wiped out, these two rear guards would be able to return to the town and let the deputy general know what had happened.

Usually, Houston always made sure he himself was part of the rear guard.

After all, this was supposed to be Judith's mission. Houston, as a vital army general, ought to have been protected. But Bash was there. So the option of sending the party ahead without him while he waited in a safe place was not currently available to Houston.

"..."

Houston had forgotten something, though.

The green soldiers were one thing, but Judith, too, was an absolute amateur of a rookie knight, who had only been in active service for around a year at that point.

All of them had enlisted during peacetime and had never tasted a real battle.

There were two other important things Houston didn't even realize.

First, that his subordinate soldiers leaned more toward loyalty to the rookie knight than to him.

And second, that after seeing how Houston had kowtowed to the opinions of an orc, his men had started to harbor a deep resentment toward him, their general...

Around that same time, Zell was pleading for their life.

"I swear, I was just passing by! You know, a little spur-of-the-moment, just-for-the-heck-of-it solo fairy trip? Well, I happened to spot this lovely looking cave, and I thought it would be just the perfect spot to explore during my adventures! Never did I dream that it would have already been inhabited by you fine fellows! All I can do is apologize for intruding on your abode! At any rate, please don't kill me... Ah... In fact...how about letting me join your gang? See, I'm a fairy, and I can provide fairy dust and...and other stuff! Yes, fairy dust! And other stuff! You fellows like fairy dust, don'cha?!"

Zell had been captured by the bandits after entering the cave, as predicted. Now the little fairy was surrounded and talking a mile a minute.

The bandits all wore matching expressions of bewilderment.

They had quickly noticed the fairy's dim glow in the blackness of the cave and immediately captured it. That had been an hour ago, and the fairy hadn't stopped talking since.

The bandits were used to hearing people plead for their lives, but the way the fairy groveled had started to actually melt their cold hearts. Despite being wrapped up in a neat little roll of cloth, Zell had managed to wriggle over to them like a caterpillar and actually kissed the tops of their feet.

Before Zell had met Bash, the fairy had another nickname, one not widely known. That nickname was Zell the Mercy Beggar.

In fact, Zell had once actually managed to escape unscathed from someone known as Gordon the Fairy Eater.

The sight of Zell pleading for mercy would sway the hearts of even the cruelest enemy.

It was one of the tricks Zell had relied on to make it through the war alive.

"Hmm, no need to go ahead and kill the little fairy now, is there?"

"There's the fairy dust to consider, too."

"And we might get cursed if we kill it."

The bandits all looked around at one another, gauging one another's feelings on the matter.

Despite their extreme hairiness, it was plain to see they were all humans.

Humans had long held a superstition about being cursed if they killed a fairy.

That, coupled with the obvious benefits of the medicinal fairy dust, made killing Zell a foolish option.

"So come on, fellas, what say you untie these wrappings and I'll shake some fairy dust all over you! Happy fairy dust will give you a nice serotonin boost, y'know!"

"Don't be absurd. We're not untying you."

Zell's request fell on deaf ears.

Fairies were tricksy little creatures. The humans knew Zell would bolt the moment the wrappings were unrolled.

The generally agreed-upon method of long-term fairy confinement was to stuff them into a small cage or bottle.

"Now, now, fellas. Truly, if I wasn't wrapped up like this, I could produce a whole mountain of fairy dust for ya! I'm talking heaps! You know, back in the day, they might as well have called me the Dust Storm!"

Zell feared the cage and the bottle.

So to avoid them, the fairy always tried to buddy up to their captors. That way, they might go a little easier, or so Zell hoped. Usually, the results were mixed, though.

"Oi! What are you all doing?"

From behind the bandits came a deep, throaty voice.

In unison, the bandits all turned around.

"It's the chief!"

The bandits sounded delighted.

They parted to allow the owner of the voice to pass, and the looming figure came into Zell's field of view.

So, this was the chief of the bandit group. He was as rough and uncultured a thug as Zell had ever seen.

Meaty arms, a huge mouth, sharp eyes.

Dressed in crudely put together leather clothing, he also wore a necklace made out of skulls, which was extremely unstylish and in rather poor taste.

The main feature that was immediately apparent, however, was his skin. It was green.

Yes, green skin. And two long, strong tusks rising from his huge mouth.

The chief was an orc.

"Oh! Oh!"

The instant Zell laid eyes on the orc, something sparked in the fairy's memory. With just a glimpse of that hulking figure, Zell knew who this was.

It was truly only a glimpse in the dank light of the cave. But that was enough. Still, Zell couldn't recall the orc's name. Zell only remembered what he looked like after encountering him on the battlefield.

"General! It's you, isn't it?! Long time no see! It's me! Zell! Zell the fairy!"

Incidentally, Zell had always been terrible at remembering names. Faces, too.

The only orc Zell could reliably recognize was Bash. The others all sort of blurred together. The fairy certainly hadn't bothered to remember this orc's name. Generally, Zell just referred to all other orcs with vaguely honorific, all-purpose forms of address like *general* or *chief*.

"What do we have here? Bash's little fairy flunky? What're ya doin' in a place like this?"

Zell's name was widely known among orcs, though.

In fact, there wasn't an orc alive who wasn't familiar with Zell after witnessing the little fairy sticking to the Hero Bash's side like glue during the war.

"You gotta hear my story, General! So there I was, out on a trip to see the wide world after the war and all. Anyway, I came across this splendid cave! And I thought to myself, Zell, this cave just *reeks* of treasure! So in I went... But alas! The only thing that was reeking was this band of scruffy human bandits! General, you gotta help me!"

Tied up like a bagworm, Zell nonetheless tried their hardest to hop and squirm their way closer to the orc.

Zell looked undignified indeed. But the orc known as the chief recognized the fairy as an old war buddy.

Why, his life had been saved numerous times by this noisy bagworm, and by the Hero Bash.

"All right, all right. Release the fairy! We're old pals."

"Are ya sure? Fairies are notorious blabbermouths, an' this one knows all about us. If it talks..."

The orc grimaced, tusks protruding as he glared at the hesitant group of bandits.

Then he leaned his hideous face right up against Zell's and muttered in a threatening tone:

"Oi, fairy. Us bein' here is a secret, got it? Don't go tellin' no one, understand?"

"I wouldn't dream of it! Have you ever known me to spill a secret? These lips of mine are sealed up tight! Me? Blab? Never! Why, if I was the blabbermouth sort of fairy, the boss...I mean Bash...would have been killed on the battlefield long ago, leaving nothing but a statue of him to mourn over back in orc country!"

Actually, this was true. Zell had never spilled a secret.

The fairy was a blabbermouth, to be sure. But most of what they babbled about was inconsequential. Zell held a lot of pride over their ability to distinguish between sensitive information and mere word vomit.

So Zell had never spilled a genuine secret in all their life.

"All right. Untie it."

"Yessir."

The bandits nodded, still looking uneasy despite the chief's firm order. Hesitantly, they untied Zell.

Zell rolled free of the wrappings, then zoomed up into the air and straight out of the cave...but only in their mind. In reality, Zell merely flew over to the chief and began hovering expectantly in front of the orc's face.

"Thanks, General! You saved me! You are as wise as you are generously endowed! But, General, pray tell... Why are you having clandestine meetings with a bunch of humans in a place like this?"

Zell's duty was to gather information.

A freewheeling fairy though they might have been, Zell would never shirk this important duty.

"Hmph. Well. Nemesis, that traitor, is insistin' on peace with the humans! Take away fightin' from the orcs, an' what's left? Nothin'! That's what! I refuse ta go along with it! So I left orc country. An' on my travels, I ran into this band of humans, and we came ta an understandin' of sorts."

The orc looked at the bandits, who all grinned and chuckled.

"At first, I was hung up on me bein' an orc an' them bein' humans. But then I realized you can still find like-minded folk out there, even among different races."

"Fascinating! So you're here making an alliance with a mind to start a new war? Killing everyone who stands in your path along the way? Like...like...a destroyer corps?"

"Precisely! Well, actually, I'd like ta tell ya that. The truth is, it ain't goin' so well yet. Right now, we're gatherin' power in secret so the orcs an' humans don't find out about it. Then, once we're strong enough, we'll launch our full-scale operation!"

"Wow! That's amazing, General!"

Zell put on a big show of being shocked and impressed. *Now I've found out what I needed, it's time to fly,* they thought secretly, then began fluttering around the cave to get their bearings.

That's when Zell noticed multiple pairs of glimmering eyes, visible in the dark. Unknown creatures were in the cave with them.

"General! Th-there's something else in here with us!"

"Of course there is. Have ya forgotten? I'm a beast tamer, ya know."

Zell knew of the demon art of beast taming, of course.

It was a strange practice, different from magic. A dark power that even regular folk could wield, not just mages. It allowed a person to take over the minds of others and bend them to their will. One example of this practice was its use in taming otherwise wild and unruly creatures...

"You're in command of the bugbears!"

Several gears had begun to click into place in the fairy's tiny brain. The name of the hulking orc came back to Zell at that moment.

This orc's name was Boggs. He was one of eight great chiefs who had survived the war.

Yes, Beast Master Boggs. He had commanded a herd of around a hundred bugbears in the war, which he used to slay hundreds of thousands of humans. It was a bloodbath.

Of course, he did more in the war than just command bugbears. He was as strong a soldier as any other orc and wielded a steel mace, which he used to smash hundreds of enemies into bloody bags of meat and bone.

Indeed, the warrior Boggs was a formidable fighter, who'd fought for forty long years on the battlefield.

"Sadly, the original flock of bugbears I raised from cubs has seriously decreased in number..."

Boggs cast a tender, loving glance over at the bugbears that were snuggled together in a corner of the cave.

During the war, Boggs's flock of bugbears had exceeded a hundred in number.

He'd commanded more bugbears than any other orc.

During the final stages of the war, Boggs's bugbears had been almost wiped out in a series of crushing defeats. He was left with only a tiny flock, numbering less than ten.

But Zell could clearly make out a dozen or so bugbears relaxing in the dark cave.

Only a few of their number were the sort of robust and muscular bugbears that would be suitable for battle.

The others looked as though only a few years had elapsed since they'd been tamed. It was clear that their bodies were much weaker and punier than the battle-ready bugbear specimens. Boggs's bugbears were always said to be stronger than the ogres and smarter than the lizardmen, the pride of the orc army.

"For now, anyway. They're growin' fast in number. Soon, I'll have taught this lot how ta tame as well, an' we'll set about makin' us the strongest fightin' corps there ever was!"

When Zell looked closer, they realized that several of the bugbears were extremely small, about the same size as the fairy.

Bugbear cubs. It took about six months for bugbears to go from cubs to mature adults.

Actually seeing a real live bugbear cub was an extremely rare thing.

"Once that happens, I'll reign as Orc King, an' we'll take on the world as our enemies!"

The human bandits all clapped, showing their appreciation for Boggs's grandiose speech. One could even be heard to yell, *"Hail to the chief!"*

To Zell's eyes, it actually didn't look like the bandits were totally on board with this master plan.

In fact, it looked more like they were just along for the ride, in it for whatever they could get.

"Grawr..."

Suddenly, the bugbears began to growl.

The sound made Boggs and all the bandits leap to attention and grab their weapons.

"What's up?"

"Intruders! Hop to it, men!" Boggs roared, grabbing his iron mace and dashing off somewhere in the darkness.

The bugbears and the bandits followed suit. They had clearly tasted battle before and were swift to leap to action.

The lights in the cave disappeared then.

The only light remaining came from the mellow glow emitted by Zell, who had been left all alone in the dark cave.

With no one to guard the fairy, this was surely their cue to escape.

And yet Zell was curious about these so-called intruders.

If it was Bash who had launched an attack on the cave, then something was very odd indeed.

"Darn it! Where are they comin' from?!"

"Hey, there's a woman! A woman, I say!"

"Someone get the lamp... Gahhh!"

"Who hit me? Who?!"

"How should I know? It's too dark to see anythin'! Gah!"

"Someone light the cursed lamp already!"

The sound of battle soon filled the cave. But oddly, there was no clanging of sword upon sword. Just a series of dull thuds and plenty of shrieks.

There was a fight going on, that was for certain. But Bash was not among their number. If Bash had been there, the sounds of carnage would have been so much squelchier and more violent.

From the sounds of things alone, Zell knew Bash wasn't there. Nevertheless, the little fairy decided to stay put for a few minutes more.

Often, Zell had adopted a similar policy during the war.

There had been many occasions when hanging back instead of leaping into the fray had served the fairy well.

"All right..."

Zell zoomed up into the air.

Scouting for information was the important thing here. Even in the pitch-dark, Zell might be able to find out something of value.

But when Zell arrived at the scene of the battle, the fight was over, the area lit by a burning torch.

Under the dim, flickering light of the torch, Zell could see the wounded forms of the soldiers. Right in the middle, bleeding from the head and with both hands bound, lay Judith.

"...What happened here?"

"There ya are, Zell. As ya can see...some knights from the local area came bustin' in an' tried ta subdue us."

"Ah, I... I see..."

Judith turned her head and looked up at Zell.

Yikes! the fairy thought, quickly trying to hide from Judith's view. Zell was worried Judith might say something that would make it obvious Zell had gone ahead as their scout.

However, despite looking surprised for a moment, Judith soon narrowed her eyes at Zell with a look of distaste.

The meaning of her sudden change in facial expression was lost on Zell.

But this was the woman whom Bash had his eye on. Zell had to make sure she wasn't killed.

"Look what else flew into our net after the fairy! An' a fine piece of meat she is, at that!"

"Geh-heh-heh... Chief, how about givin' the woman over ta me?"

"Idiot! We're all gonna share her, right, brothers?"

"Right, right, no keepin' the lady all to yourself."

"All right, how's this? We lock up the woman, kill all the men, an' then dump their bodies outside."

Judith's face suddenly seemed to drain of all color.

"Guh... Just...kill me..."

Judith sounded brave, but her expression was one of abject terror. Her eyes were darting all over the place, and there was a chattering sound coming from her jaw. Every so often, there was a *glop, glop* sound as she gulped hard. She looked like she was about to burst into tears at any second.

Aha, this could go in my favor.

Zell saw this as a golden opportunity.

This knight was, to put it mildly, completely screwed. If Zell could somehow engineer a heroic rescue, Bash's stock would shoot sky-high.

Indeed, it might even be enough to make the female knight fall head over heels in love.

"Hey! Not so fast! There's no sense in killing them now! Not when you've made it this far without your operation being exposed! If the townsfolk discover the bodies, you'll find yourselves hounded and hunted down by scores of knights!"

The bandits all turned scornful, mocking eyes on Zell.

But Zell barely even flinched. Because Zell was a fairy, and they have next to zero social awareness.

"I know just what you should do! Wait until morning and then execute them outside! Stage it so it looks like they finally found the bugbears they were seeking. *Oh, whoops, we were in pursuit, and then just outside the forest, bam! Bugbear attack! Blood everywhere!* Oh, and you should leave a few bugbear corpses just so it looks like it was a real fight to the death. Humans are stupid; they'll totally buy it! Look, do you really want all your good work to go to waste? No, no, it would be such a shame! I know you're too smart, too cunning to blow the whole thing now! Not to mention, it's really dark in here. Don'cha wanna take a good look at their faces in daylight while you kill 'em? See that look in their eyes that says *This can't be happening!...?* It's gonna feel *so* much more satisfying to kill 'em while drinking in that look, don'cha think?"

As Zell's barrage of word vomit rained down upon the bandits, they actually seemed to be considering it. Their faces said, *Hmm, maybe the fairy's got a point?*

After all, they could kill them anytime they wanted, right?

They had time on their side, and their position was still safe, wasn't it?

Zell's words had a strange power, a power to make them all feel secure and confident. In certain circles, Zell had yet another nickname. This one was Honey-Tongued Zell. Once Zell started flattering, cajoling, and convincing, it was hard for anyone to resist.

"Ya may have a point, fairy. All right, men. We lock 'em all up. Heh, Lady Knight...I'm gonna take ya all the way ta heaven while my men watch..."

After some thought, that was the conclusion Boggs came to.

Grabbing the female knight by the hair, Boggs dragged her off deeper into the cave, her limp body scraping across the rough stone floor.

As she was being dragged away, Judith kept her eyes fixed on Zell. The look within them was a mixture of despair and accusation, anger over being betrayed.

Boss! I've set everything up perfectly! It's the ideal situation! If this isn't enough to get results, nothing will be! Now all that's left is for you to make a timely appearance and save the fair maiden!

Zell wasn't even looking in Judith's direction.

When Bash awoke, Houston was sitting nearby, cradling his head in his hands.

"I can't believe this... Gotta be kidding me..."

Judith and the other soldiers were nowhere to be seen.

"What happened to the others?"

Houston lifted his head at the sound of Bash's voice. His expression was one of guilt.

"This is embarrassing, but...it looks like we've had a sleeping spell cast on us. The others...went on ahead."

A sleeping spell.

Magic used to put someone into an incredibly deep sleep for a short period of time.

"Did you give the order to go in?"

"No, I didn't... They mutinied."

"Mutiny? Humans defy a commanding officer's orders?"

"Sometimes. When they don't agree with them."

Bash was seriously shocked. Culture shocked.

In orc society, anyone who violated an official order was punished by death or banishment.

That was how much value orcs placed on honoring the chain of command. An official order was basically a law.

"What is the punishment for such transgressions in human society?"

"Uh, usually a lecture or a pay cut. Sometimes, depending on the circumstances, a period of self-reflection, or loss of privileges that come with being a knight."

"It doesn't sound like it's treated as a serious crime at all."

"Well, it's peacetime... Besides, widespread incompetence has become relatively common among the human leadership. A lot of folks are opposed to the concept of blindly going along with incompetent orders and getting killed. Ah, I'm so embarrassed. I suppose I'm one to talk, huh?"

"Hmm."

Bash didn't care whether Houston was incompetent or not.

Nor did he care about the laughably lax human treatment of the heinous crime of mutiny, shocked as he was to hear about it.

The more important thing right now was the stench of blood that Bash had already noticed was wafting out of the cave.

Judith, the prime wife candidate Bash had set his heart on, had gone into that cave. He couldn't shake the thought that she might be in terrible danger.

"So what now?"

"Well, the sleeping spell has worn off, but the troops still haven't returned. That's not good. It's likely they've all been killed already. We should return to the town and gather reinforcements..."

"Such weakness of spirit is not what this occasion requires."

Bash glared at Houston.

The woman he had his eye on might be in serious danger. There was no way Bash was about to retreat.

"But you are the officer in charge. If you issue a command, I shall follow it."

Orcs always obeyed commands.

However, they were free to question a commanding officer's judgment at any time. It was largely frowned upon, but Bash felt it was warranted in the current situation.

"Just one thing, though. Orcs are never cowards. We follow rules, but then we give our all to the battle."

Houston blinked, gazing at Bash.

Green skin, long tusks, rippling muscles. Just your standard-issue, slightly smaller than average orc. But no one would ever mistake this orc for another or forget him after seeing him in action even once. During the war, Houston had felt like he was always fleeing from this very orc.

Usually, Houston would have no problem abandoning Judith in a heartbeat.

Serves her right. That's what she gets for disobeying orders. Houston wasn't foolish enough to risk his neck to save an idiot like that.

And if the townsfolk had called him a coward, he would have simply turned a deaf ear.

But Bash was right there, watching him. There was no one whom Houston feared or respected more.

Houston was proud of his conduct in the war. It was not cowardice that had led him to run from Bash. It was a calculated tactic to ensure victory. After all, Houston had survived the war, hadn't he? And the orc side had lost, hadn't they? Houston didn't want to think of himself as a coward who had only survived the war because he had been lucky in his attempts to evade Bash.

"...All right. Understood. Then we will infiltrate the cave at once, save our compatriots, and kill every last one of our foes."

"Got it."

The Orc Hero Bash exposed his long tusks in a smile.

7

JUDITH

I had a sister once.

I was so proud to have her as my sister.

There were ten years between us, so by the time I started being able to actually form memories, my sister was already a gifted student and a proper young lady, an example to everyone around her. She was the pride and hope of our family.

I grew up idolizing my sister.

In turn, she treated me with such kindness, even though I was so much younger.

Apparently she was put on a pedestal by the other kids at school and didn't have close friends as a result, so having me running around after her all the time yelling, "Big Sis, Big Sis!" really made her happy.

I used to love it when my sister would braid my hair. She was so talented and could do anything, but she was rather clumsy when it came to hair. My hair always ended up lopsided, leaning to one side or the other. I used to love walking around with lopsided hair. I wore it like a badge of honor, a symbol of sisterly love.

After my sister graduated from school, she became a knight.

I come from a family of knights, you see, and my sister intended to follow in the family footsteps. The country was in the midst of war back then, and they needed all the troops they could get.

With her abilities, my sister rose up the ranks soon after becoming a knight. Within a few years, she was in charge of her own platoon.

Once a year, my sister would return to the family home and entertain us all with tales from the battlefield.

My sister's achievements including slaying a Demon Lord and winning countless major battles. Soon, the tides of war were turning in favor of the Alliance of Four Races. It looked like the war would be ending soon. When my sister came home last, she told me, *"Once the war's done, I'm going to focus on training you up! You're going to become a knight, too, of course. I'll start by teaching you the sword. Heh-heh. Maybe you'll even be posted to my platoon! Well, it won't be like it is at home! I'll make sure to work you hard!"*

Yes…that's what she said, a big smile on her face.

But then, just a few months later, my sister's platoon was wiped out. She was taken captive by the orcs and held as a prisoner of war.

The news devastated my family.

Father and Mother's faces fell, as if the world were ending. They said terrible things, like how it would be better if my sister had just died.

I didn't understand at the time. How could my parents say such a thing?

This was my sister they were talking about. Both Father and Mother had absolutely doted on her.

I remember screaming at them, *"How dare you say that about your own daughter! You're despicable!"* Then I locked myself up in my room.

I didn't speak to either of my parents for a long time after that.

Then a few years passed.

The war ended.

The Alliance of Four Races, to which the humans belonged, had won the war. The Coalition of Seven Races, to which the orcs belonged, had lost.

The orcs' prisoners of war were all released.

My sister came home, too.

That's when I realized what it really meant for a woman to be taken captive by the orcs.

My sister was…defiled.

She was dead behind the eyes, her hair a matted bird's nest. She had always had perfect posture, but now she scuttled about, bent over and hunchbacked, as if trying to hide herself from sight.

She barely spoke, and if any men came near, she would shriek and shake.

Even if that man was our own father.

I heard later that my sister had been forced to wed a great orc chief, and she bore him six children by the time the war finally ended.

Being pregnant and giving birth so many times over such a short period completely wrecked my sister's body and mental health. She returned a shell of a person, utterly unsuitable for continuing her career as a knight.

At the same time, she was far too damaged for remarrying.

My sister's future, her life…it was all ruined. Forever.

I vowed revenge on the orcs.

I'm not stupid. I understand how things work. The orc race…that's just how they are. They see things differently to us. They don't share our values. Orcs follow their own customs, just like cats seek out dark, tight spaces and dogs look for trees to piss on. The orcs did what they did not out of malice, but simply because it was their way.

But there's a difference between logic and emotion.

I wanted to kill every last orc with my bare hands.

And so I became a knight.

Of course, that was always the plan. But now I was more determined than ever.

The war ended, and the army was cut back drastically. The demand for knights decreased, too. It took me a while, but I finally made it and became a knight anyway.

The Fortified City of Krassel was my top choice for placement.

Krassel was the closest town to orc country. If war broke out again, it would be the first town to taste combat against the orcs. Also, Houston the Pig Slayer was stationed there.

My placement request was granted.

Many around me expressed concern about me, a female knight, going so close to orc country. I ignored them all.

Meanwhile, Houston the Pig Slayer was everything people said he was.

He was merciless in his dealings with the rogue orcs that came out of the orc country.

He would interrogate them to find out why they had been banished. But whatever they said, Houston did not care.

He executed them all, no matter what they claimed or how much they protested. Orcs that had committed known criminal acts, orcs with perfect conduct...Houston executed them all the same.

Houston's logic made perfect sense to me. *Banished orcs have already committed crimes in their own country. It doesn't matter if they've behaved perfectly on human soil so far. They're still criminals. There's no point waiting around for them to commit crimes in our land, too. Then it would be too late.*

When I saw how ruthless Houston was in his attitude toward the orcs, I made up my mind to follow him.

After the war, everyone was focused on trying to get to know other races and learn about their mindsets and customs. But not Houston. He was brutal toward the orcs. I loved that.

I knew if I stuck with Houston, the revenge I sought would come to me someday. I wanted to kill them all, every last orc.

With Houston, I had faith.

But then I learned there was an exception, a loophole in Houston's anti-orc policy. I'm talking about the non-rogue orcs.

In other words, travelers and those on special missions for their own country. Those orcs, Houston would simply question and release.

But no such orcs had come through, not since my appointment to Krassel. So I'd forgotten all about the non-rogue orcs.

Then one came to town.

The orc who went by the name Bash...he was different from any other orc I knew of.

He seemed a bit smaller physically than most orcs, but he was incredibly muscular, much more so than the others. And he was dignified.

It wasn't just the way he carried himself, either. His face was dignified, too.

The rogue orcs always seemed to be mocking you. Whenever they laid eyes on me, they always (and I mean *always*) bared their tusks in lecherous grins, raking their eyes over my breasts and butt.

I hated those looks. I hated them so much! But at least Bash hadn't leered at me.

Yes, he checked out my chest and my butt. But so what? So did all the human men. That wasn't a big deal. Sure, it was kinda gross, but whatever.

My problem was with Houston, though, and the way he started acting ever since Bash showed up.

Honestly, I was left a bit disillusioned.

I mean, what the heck was that all about? And what happened to the Pig Slayer?

It seemed like this orc, Bash, was somebody important back in his own country.

I got that, all right. But there was no need for Houston to simper and fawn over him like that. I mean...the guy was only an orc.

Then after that, Houston announced that we were all going to search the forest together. And he kept asking for Bash's opinion on literally everything.

It was obvious Houston was desperate not to lose face with the orc, for whatever reason. That's why he was making such a big show out of trying to solve the highway ambush case.

I was getting more and more suspicious by the minute.

That's why I mutinied and went against orders. It was purely based on my own instincts. Just a bit of childish rebellion.

But no, it was more than that.

It was because my sister was kept as a slave for years and broken in both body and spirit.

Even if defeat was inevitable, and the defilement of my sister was an unavoidable consequence, perhaps some of my sister could still have been salvaged if only she'd been rescued sooner.

That's why I felt so strongly about launching immediate rescue missions to retrieve prisoners of war.

Even though this time, the prisoner of war was a fairy who meant nothing to me whatsoever.

The soldiers, who knew my backstory, were all too happy to align with me.

Even if we betrayed orders, it wouldn't matter in the end if the mission ended favorably. Sure, we might all be facing pay cuts or forced periods of self-reflection, but we'd get away with it otherwise. Honestly, we were all way too flippant about the whole thing.

We didn't consider the implications of our actions or the true meaning of Houston's orders. And we underestimated the strength of our enemy.

"Guh-heh-heh... Can't wait until tomorrow."

As a result of our hubris, the lives of myself and my soldiers now seemed to hang by a thread.

"Guh..."

"Ugh..."

We were all tied up, lying on the cold, hard ground.

Everyone had incurred heavy injuries. Some had broken bones; some were unconscious.

No one had been killed, not yet, but a few men had lost huge amounts of blood and would be cold and stiff come morning.

It was only by sheer luck that the battle had ended without any of us losing our lives outright.

We'd been ambushed the moment we infiltrated the cave.

First, they targeted our lights.

In the darkness of the cave, it was impossible to tell how many enemies there were. One by one, we fell.

In the aftermath of the battle, we found ourselves lying at the feet of about a dozen or so humans and an equivalent number of bugbears.

Oh, and one orc.

Yes...an *orc*.

And not just any orc, either. A beast tamer.

As I glared up at him with hatred, he leered at me with a lecherous, mocking expression on his hideous face.

Fear seized hold of me.

"Look what else flew into our net after the fairy! An' a fine piece of meat she is, at that!"

"Geh-heh-heh... Chief, how about givin' the woman over ta me?"

"Idiot! We're all gonna share her, right, brothers?"

"Right, right, no keepin' the lady all to yourself."

"All right, how's this? We lock up the woman, kill all the men, an' then dump their bodies outside."

When I heard that, I suddenly knew what they had in store for me.

"Guh... Just...kill me..."

I could hear the fear in my own weak, tremulous voice.

I knew I didn't want to die, though. I still hadn't really done anything yet. What was the point of me going through all that to become a knight just to die now? I couldn't stand the thought of it. *Please... Don't do anything to me, please.*

That's when I heard a high-pitched little voice in the dimness.

"Hey! Not so fast! There's no sense in killing them now! Not when you've made it this far without your operation being discovered! If the townsfolk discover the bodies, you'll find yourselves hounded and hunted down by scores of knights!"

The little creature was hovering in the air, emitting a mild glow that was visible in the gloom.

"I know just what you should do! Wait until morning and then execute them outside! Stage it so it looks like they finally found the bugbears they were seeking. *Oh, whoops, we were in pursuit, and then just outside the forest, bam! Bugbear attack! Blood everywhere!* Oh, and you should leave a few bugbear corpses just so it looks like it was a real fight to the death. Humans are stupid; they'll totally buy it! Look, do you really want all your good work to go to waste? No, no, it would be such a shame! I know you're too smart, too cunning to blow the whole thing now! Not to mention, it's really dark in here. Don'cha wanna take a good look at their faces in daylight while you kill 'em? See that look in their eyes that says *This can't be happening!...?*" It's gonna feel *so* much more satisfying to kill 'em while drinking in that look, don'cha think?"

It was Zell.

I couldn't believe it.

I'd assumed the fairy had simply gotten itself captured, but no. The evil little thing had been on the side of this group of bandits all along.

The ambush we walked right into, which was no doubt set up based on the intel the wretched fairy had provided.

"Ya may have a point, fairy. All right, men. We lock 'em all up. Heh, Lady Knight...I'm gonna take ya all the way ta heaven while my men watch..."

The orc grabbed hold of my hair and yanked me along, dragging me deeper into the cave.

My ears were filled with the horrible sound of the bandits all laughing and jeering as I was taken away.

◆

In the depths of the cave, I was dragged to a room with nothing else in it but a dirty straw mattress. Then I was thrown roughly to the floor.

I turned to see the orc looming above me. Just one orc.

The rest were all humans.

They were hairy and unkempt and looked like a bunch of dirty bandits. Still, they were unmistakably human.

"You vile scoundrels... How could you team up with a filthy orc? Have you no sense of human pride?"

"A *filthy* orc? Now, now, that's just racist. The war's over, y'know. We're all on the same side now. We gotta play nice together...right?"

At this, the bandits all burst out laughing, and with calls of "Hear, hear!" began slapping the orc on the shoulder.

The orc grinned in amusement as well and began slapping the bandits' shoulders right back.

I was in so much more trouble than I ever realized.

It had never crossed my mind that orcs and humans might team up.

Thinking about it logically, though, it actually wasn't so strange.

Taming wild animals was an old demon technique, widely adopted by the orcs. And bugbears were one of the most common animals that were manipulated this way.

We learned this in knight school.

So there were more than a few orcs around who would be capable of orchestrating the recent bugbear attacks. Orc country was close by, too. It all made sense.

But orcs didn't have the sophistication to attack merchants and abscond with just the right amount of loot to avoid raising suspicion.

If an orc attacked a merchant by their own designs, they would simply plunder everything and leave nothing behind, not even scraps.

If they were benefiting from the sophisticated touch of humans, then that would be a different story, however...

Why hadn't I figured this out sooner? It was so obvious.

Well, I knew why.

Because I was acting under the delusion that humans and orcs would never team up. That orcs weren't *capable* of forming true alliances with other races.

And I really believed that the superior human race would never sink so low as to fraternize with orcs.

Now look where my naïveté had led me.

"All right, who's first? It's gotta be the chief, right?"

"No, no. You all have your fun first. I'll go after."

"Ya can't be serious, Chief. Lady knights are a favorite among orcs, ain't they?"

"It's orc custom to let the lower-rankers have the first go."

"Well, it's *human* custom to defer to the boss. We wouldn't 'ave gotten this far without your bugbears, Chief."

"Oh yeah? What's that y'all sayin' about hatin' authority an' never bowin' down to the higher-ups?"

"It's a different story when it's someone we respect, Chief. We all trust ya, y'know."

"Heh-heh. Well, if that's the case, then I don't mind if I do."

The orc reached for me with his horrible, meaty hands.

He was going to defile me, just like my sister. The realization was horrible and absolute. I could feel all the blood drain from my face.

My hands and feet had gone cold, and I was starting to shake.

"N-no...! Stop...!"

"Now, now, Miss Knight, that ain't the right attitude, is it? Considerin' the situation yer in, don'cha wanna beg for death instead? It would make it so much more interestin'. What about whatcha said before? Let's hear that one again, hmm?"

"No! No, no, no!!!"

All I could think about was my sister, broken beyond repair.

In my mind, I could still hear her screaming in terror whenever our father got too close. Our own father. I could still see her face, the horrible empty look in her eyes as she told us about the six orc children she'd been forced to bear...

I was enraged. It was the orcs that did this to her. I knew I would have to dedicate my life to wiping out every last one.

When I was forced to look upon Bash's...*engorgement*...I felt no sense of embarrassment nor hysteria. No, I felt nothing but pure, burning rage.

I had never imagined anything worse than that happening to me.

I was so naive. Never in my wildest dreams did I think the atrocities my sister endured might one day befall me.

"Get off me! No! No! No! No!!!"

"Hey! Settle down, will ya?"

With my hands tied behind my back, it was impossible for me to prevent the orc from yanking off my armor with a series of heavy *clanks*.

All I could do was sob and scream.

Once my armor was off, all the men leaned in closer, eyes drinking in the contours of my body, now visible through my tight-fitting cotton undergarment.

"I can't wait any longer!"

"Nooo!!!"

The orc's hands reached out and tore my undergarment right down the front. The sound of the other men's heavy breathing suddenly increased. Drool began to drip from one corner of the orc's foul mouth.

"...Oi! What's that sound?"

One of the men suddenly yelped, looking concerned.

"What?"

The men stopped panting all of a sudden, and silence filled the room. The sound of fighting was suddenly audible, coming from somewhere close by.

Actually, it wasn't *exactly* like the sound of a fight. It was more like the sound of one person smashing their way through, unchallenged.

Just then, one of the other men came dashing into the room, tripping over his own feet in a panic.

"Chief! It's the enemy!"

"What?! There were more of 'em? How many?!"

"It's...it's just two..."

"What?! Then pull yerself together an' deal with it! Don't let 'em get away!"

Just two? That was of no interest to these bandits.

The men were more concerned with the matter at hand. They were all about to get a turn enjoying a woman for the first time in who knew how long. They all returned their eyes to me, hungrily.

Some still seemed concerned by the panicked appearance of the messenger, though.

Upon closer inspection, his face was spattered with blood, but the complexion underneath was pale and sickly.

The messenger yelled out again.

"There's no one left ta deal with it! They darn near wiped us all out! We hafta run, now..."

That's when the wall suddenly exploded.

All the bandits froze and turned to look in the direction of the disturbance.

From the cloud of dust, a tiny glowing creature came bobbing through the air.

"Ah, nice job, Boss! You were right on the money."

The fairy sounded calm and relaxed, so different from the hyperactive chatter it had been coming out with earlier.

The dust cloud gradually settled.

There was a huge hole yawning open in the wall.

Then, from that gaping hole, a hulking figure stepped into the room.

The sight of the figure stole away my last shreds of hope.

Green skin, long tusks. Another orc. As if one wasn't bad enough.

I began to tremble even harder than ever before.

Just picturing what was about to happen to me made my limbs go numb with fear. I could feel tears streaming down my cheeks.

Resignation flooded me, and I accepted my fate...

"..."

But the new orc looked around the room, finally fixing its eyes on me.

It wasn't leering at my exposed, naked skin. No, this orc looked me right in the eyes.

Then it spoke in a voice I'd come to recognize over the past few days.

"I'm here to help."

...That's what the orc said.

8

THE HERO VS. THE COMMANDER OF THE BEASTS

The cave was cramped and claustrophobic.

The roof was around ten feet from the ground, and the passageways were around six feet wide.

It was a tight fit for an orc but quite roomy for a human. In all likelihood, this cave had been used by the orcs as a frontline base position during the war.

But even Bash, for all his wartime experience, did not know about it.

It must have been abandoned over twenty years ago, at least.

Until the bandits found it and made it their hideout.

It only took a surprisingly short amount of time to reach Judith.

After entering the cave and reaching an open chamber of sorts, Bash had swiftly dealt with the lookout guards. Then Zell came zooming up at top speed, jabbering with excitement.

"Boss! You sure took your sweet time! This way! Quickly, quickly! Right now, this moment, this second, your lady knight is on the cusp of being ravished and devoured! This is your cue to mount a dashing rescue! But if you don't hurry, it'll be too late! You must hurry, Boss! Hurry! In fact, I recommend bashing through that wall and making your own shortcut!"

Houston remained in the cavern, saying that he would secure the exit and deal with any enemy stragglers.

In Bash's opinion, Houston had more than adequate training.

Even if they did have backup, he could handle a few bandits alone.

Now, right before Bash's very eyes was the woman he'd had his eye on for days, half-naked and exposed.

Bash's little warrior perked up immediately at the sight of her. *Boss! Now's the time!* it seemed to say as it rose stiffly from between Bash's legs. But Bash ignored it.

If Houston had been there, he would have surely been surprised by the sight.

An orc confronted with the sight of a naked woman and yet restraining the beast within.

What a hero, Houston may have thought.

Of course, Judith wasn't the only one in the room.

There was also another orc and several human bandits.

"Whaddaya want? Hey, it's an orc. This a friend of yours, Chief?"

"Ya came to help, huh? Too late, we already dealt with all the soldiers."

The bandits all shot Bash quizzical looks, but none of them seemed very alarmed by his entrance.

Instead, they seemed curious as to the identity of this strange orc who had come bursting through the wall all of a sudden. The bandits turned to their leader inquisitively.

"Chief, who is this?"

"Wh-what...? What...?"

But their orc leader's green skin had gone a sickly blue shade. He'd turned into a blue orc.

Shaky and trembling, all he seemed to be able to say was "Wh-what?" as he stared wide-eyed at Bash.

He knew that face.

"Is that you, Boggs?"

"Eek!"

Boggs.

Yes, Bash knew who Boggs was, too.

Boggs was an orc soldier—a beast tamer—who'd commanded a group of bugbears during the war.

He was the only orc who had attained the title of beast master.

But Boggs was never able to accept the peace treaty with the humans and had openly opposed the Orc King. As a result, he was one of the rogue ones cast out of orc country.

"Boggs, it is forbidden for orcs to force themselves upon women. We must first obtain their consent."

"I... I was just... I wasn't forcing meself! She wanted me ta do it!"

"...Bullshit."

Judith's face was caked with snot and tears, and she was desperately trying to conceal her womanly parts from view.

If this was what consent looked like, then Bash could have already disposed of his virginity with those two merchant women he first met in the forest.

"Hey, Chief... We all thought this was a friend of yours, but from the way he's talkin' to ya, it's clear he's the enemy, yeah?"

One of the bandits drew his sword, then with a smug, condescending smile, came rushing at Bash.

His eyes were filled with the intent to kill.

"Good guess."

Bash nodded, answering in a mild tone.

There was no need for denial or subterfuge of any kind.

"Then die!"

The bandit was quick on his feet.

Raising his sword to chest height, he thrust at Bash, aiming for the orc's eye.

He was nothing more than a bandit now, but he'd actually been in the war and survived. Comfortable fighting in confined spaces, he was also quite skilled with the sword.

"That big fancy weapon won't do ya much good in here!"

The bandit thrust his sword forward, expecting to deal a killing blow.

But just as he could perfectly visualize his sword tip piercing Bash's eye and sending forth freshets of blood...his own head exploded in a spray of jelly and bone, and he fell to the floor, dead.

"Huh?"

None of the other bandits could process what had just happened.

Their comrade's head had disappeared with a ridiculous popping sound, just as he was leaping to attack the enemy.

That much they had seen with their own eyes. But the logistics of it didn't make any sense.

"What?"

One among their number noticed what had occurred, however.

The orc's sword had left its scabbard and was now held loosely in one hand.

The greatsword had been on the right, and then it was on the left. But how could Bash have swung his greatsword in the cramped confines of the cave?

A second later, the cave wall around Bash exploded with a roar of sound.

It was like the sword had eaten its way through the walls.

"Whoa!"

The bandits all cowered and screamed as the walls exploded.

Bash's sword swing had eaten its way through the very walls of the cave before cleaving the attacking bandit's head clean in two.

That was what had happened.

The rubble now tumbling all over the cave was the only visible sign of Bash's swing.

The bandits were too panicked to process what Bash had done, though. All they knew was that their comrade was dead, and the walls had exploded. All they could do was cower in terror. They had all frozen up completely. They didn't even realize they were standing within attack range themselves.

His expression grim, Bash swung his greatsword for a second time.

The trembling group of bandits were all swiftly separated from the lower halves of their bodies.

They never even had time to cry out.

All of the bandits now lay in multiple different pieces in puddles of their own blood. None of them ever even knew what had hit them.

"...Crap!"

The only one left alive was Boggs, who had witnessed Bash in action at close quarters before.

Boggs was the only one who had understood that tight spaces were no hindrance to Bash. He realized that Bash's sword would crash through the walls and decimate the unsuspecting bodies of the bandits.

As a result, Boggs was the only one who had thought to back out of range of Bash's swing.

"Why? Why did ya hafta come here?!"

Bellowing loudly, Boggs suddenly darted away, running out of the room and heading for the cave's exit.

As Bash took a step forward to follow him, Zell whispered something rapidly in his ear, and the orc came to a sudden halt.

Then, slowly, he turned to Judith.

He was panting hard.

Well, obviously. Right on the floor in front of him lay a mostly naked woman, hands tied tightly together so that she had no way to conceal her body from his view.

"Yeek!"

Judith gulped hard.

It was only Judith and Bash left in the room now.

A half-naked woman and an orc standing at full attention. Oh, there was the fairy, too, flittering around near Bash's shoulder, emitting a mild glow.

So the fairy wasn't in cahoots with the bandits after all. But Judith knew the little thing wasn't on *her* side. From the very beginning, the fairy had been loyal only to Bash.

The fairy leaned in and began whispering something in Bash's ear.

Judith was certain it was saying something like *Now's your chance to do her, Boss!*

Perhaps this had been their plan all along, right from the very beginning.

Judith's nerves had been stretched to their breaking point, and she was ready to believe the entire world was conspiring against her.

Bash slowly reached toward Judith.

"No! Get away! I... Huh?"

Bash was making no attempt to touch Judith's bare skin.

Instead, he covered her pale, exposed flesh up with the heavy overcoat he himself had been wearing.

"...Huh?"

"I came to help you. I'll untie you. Then you should use some of this on the fallen soldiers in the jail area. It's fairy dust."

Bash undid Judith's restraints and handed her a tiny bottle.

Judith knew all about fairy dust, of course.

It was valuable stuff. A fairy could only make a certain amount of it per day.

This dust must have come from the fairy that was currently squirming with embarrassment somewhere near Bash's ear.

That's when it finally clicked for Judith.

The orc had come here to save her.

She was being saved.

Rescued, in other words, from that terrifying situation.

She was not going to end up like her sister.

"You should be grateful, y'know! Our plan...I mean, *the Boss's* plan... If I hadn't gone ahead as a spy, you'd be the meat in an orc-bandit sandwich right about now!"

"I...I *am* grateful!"

Judith was blushing bright red but couldn't deny her gratitude.

It wasn't just lip service. Bash had saved not just her life, but her very spirit.

At the same time, though, Judith was surprised.

How could an orc look upon a naked woman and not do anything?

Perhaps Bash was impotent? But no, even now, Bash's excitement was visible, the bulge in his crotch region all too apparent.

In other words, Bash had suppressed his own lustful desires and put Judith's well-being above all else.

"But..."

"What is it? I've already opened up a hole in the jail wall. It's the first on your left."

"I...I already got that! It's just...why aren't you ravishing me?"

"Do you...*want* me to ravish you?"

"What?! N-no!"

Judith pulled the heavy overcoat tighter around her.

She was suddenly trembling again, recalling her terror from just before.

"But I thought that orcs loved capturing women of other races and...impregnating them?"

"We do. But the Orc King himself has forbidden nonconsensual acts of coitus with females of different races."

How many times had she heard that phrase over the past few days?

He was like a simpleton repeating himself over and over.

She'd been convinced he was all talk.

But suddenly, Judith was hit with a wave of emotion.

She understood now.

Yes...

This was *loyalty*.

That display of strength a moment ago...punching through walls, leaving a Bash-shaped impression. Taking on and killing six grown men simultaneously. With strength like that, the orc could have taken any woman he wanted. When Judith had him surrounded in the inn, he could have pulverized all the soldiers and had his way with her without even breaking a sweat.

But he hadn't. Because he was loyal. To the Orc King. He'd restrained himself.

Yes...it all made sense now. That was why Houston held the orc in such high regard.

As a great orc of the orc country. As a skilled orc warrior.

He was on par with even the leader of the knights of the royal capital.

Just as Judith was starting to understand everything, Bash turned to leave.

"Wh-where are you going?"

"After the orc."

Bash had his orders from Houston. To *"kill every last one."* He intended to perform his duty as commanded.

Houston was not Bash's lord, but he was the commanding officer of this area.

And an orc always obeys orders from the officer in charge.

"I see... That's why you..."

But Judith had come to a different interpretation of Bash's words.

She respected Bash's sense of loyalty. As a result, she now thought she had a pretty good idea what Bash was doing there.

Why Bash had come to the human country, why he had allowed the humans to detain and interrogate him, why he had joined the forest search along with the soldiers, why he had come rushing into this dark cave to save a foolish knight like her, why he was ignoring the temptations of Judith's nude female form in favor of chasing the enemy...in favor of chasing another *orc*...it all made sense to Judith now.

And now that she understood, Judith knew there was no way she was about to stand in Bash's way.

"Hmm?"

"Ah, nothing... I understand. May the fortunes of war be in your favor."

"Uh-huh."

And with that, Bash left.

Bash came across Houston on his way back through the caves, fighting in the cavern.

The human was besieged by a dozen bugbears, fighting for his life.

The cavern area was a little wider than the passageways, but it was still part of the claustrophobic cave system.

If the cramped environs weren't bad enough, taking on a dozen bugbears in such a small space seemed to be giving Houston a huge amount of trouble.

"Go forth, my bugbears! Surround the human! Kill him! Kill him now!"

Boggs was also there, screaming orders, mace in hand.

He seemed half-crazed, controlling his bugbear puppets, backing Houston into a corner.

Houston was thinking of nothing but defense and enduring the enemy's attack somehow.

If Boggs wanted to flee, it would have been better for him to ignore Houston and run. But Houston was fleet-footed and seemed to be attempting to block Boggs's escape route.

There was only one passageway leading to the exit. Only one way out.

The Boggs Bash knew should have had no problem crushing one human soldier.

And yet he could not manage it. Was it because of Houston's skills?

No, it was because Boggs was frenzied and doing a poor job of directing his bugbears.

"Boggs!"

"B-Bash?!"

Boggs whirled around at the sound of his name.

Standing there was the orc Boggs believed to be the strongest in orc country, the country he was banished from.

Wielding his greatsword, the orc Bash came walking over toward Boggs.

"Gah! Surround me!" Boggs yelled out desperately, even as he felt his blood run cold.

The bugbears all abandoned their pursuit of Houston and came to Boggs's side.

Protected by a circle of bugbears, Boggs stared Bash dead in the eye.

"Why?! ...Why have you come here?"

Bash answered him, his tone steady and even.

"I was ordered to kill you."

"Gah! So that's how it is, is it?"

Boggs understood immediately. Why Bash was here. Why the Orc Hero, who should have been resting on his laurels back in the home country, had come here to kill him.

He understood everything with only a few simple words.

Boggs may have been a rogue orc, cast out in disgrace, but he was also once a soldier.

As a beast tamer, he had experienced many battles. He was regarded with much pride by the other orcs. Yes, indeed, Boggs was everything an orc should be.

But the Orc King's orders had been at odds with Boggs's values.

No more violating unwilling women? No more fighting enemies?

How absurd! If you took away women and war from orcs, what was left? Nothing!

So Boggs had spoken out in opposition and was cast out.

But even though he had joined up with bandits, he had not abandoned his pride.

No, in his own way, Boggs always sought to uphold the values of the orc race.

But his rogue actions had been deemed distasteful by the orcs, who desired peace with the humans.

That's why the order had been given.

The order to have Boggs killed.

To have anyone who tried to disturb the peace between the orcs and the humans killed.

And who could have issued such an order?

There was only one who could have given such a command to the Hero Bash, the greatest orc of them all.

The Orc King. That wretch Nemesis had ordered Bash to take Boggs's head. For Boggs, this was the only possible answer.

"Am I really so despicable in yer eyes? Jus' fer bein' an orc who doesn't blindly follow orders?!"

Boggs knew he could never win in a fight against Bash.

His instincts were screaming at him to toss aside his mace, fall to his knees, bow his head, and beg for mercy.

But Boggs still had his pride. He hadn't lost that. Nor would he abandon his values.

How could he grovel before this man, this pride of the orcs?

How could he fall to his knees and bow before this orc, who even now was holding a sword aloft?

"I am the Beast Master Boggs of the once-mighty kingdom of the orcs!"

Boggs had spoken his name aloud.

His opponent, a Hero.

"Hmm. Then I am the Orc Hero Bash, a soldier under Captain Budarth, of the once-mighty kingdom of the orcs."

To speak aloud one's name, to unleash the standard war cry, and then to fight each other to the death...

This was the ancient custom of the orc-on-orc duel.

Boggs had offered up the challenge, and Bash had accepted. This was to be a duel between two great warriors, and the standard customs applied in this case more than they ever had.

"Graaagh!"

The cave walls shook with the force of Boggs's war cry. The sound of it made all the bugbears leap forward as one.

"Graaagh!"

Bash unleashed his own war cry in response.

The bugbears surged forward like a wave, but Bash stepped forward to meet them, showing not a single ounce of fear.

Bash's one step brought him within striking range of the bugbears.

As their heavy paws hit the ground, there was a dull flash.

Three of the bugbears were turned instantly into mincemeat.

"Gragh!!!"

Still roaring, Bash pushed forward.

With each step, one bugbear after another exploded into a spray of blood and bone.

To Bash's heavy, sharp, old reliable sword, the bugbears were little more than cattle ripe for the slaughter.

In the end, there were only five bugbears remaining.

These bugbears were seasoned fighters, ones that had survived the war. Stronger than ogres, swifter than lizardmen, Boggs's pride and joy.

"Graaagh!"

Bash took another step forward, his war cry shaking the cave walls.

His sword flashed in a storm of steel.

All orc warriors believe themselves to be the strongest.

It would be unwise to say it, but even the average soldier held the belief that he could defeat even the Orc King himself if he tried.

But even the most arrogant of orcs had to admit to themselves that they could never win in a duel against Bash.

None could evade the power of Bash's slash attack.

His sword was simply too fast, too powerful.

Boggs's eyes weren't sharp enough to follow Bash's movements. But the bugbears were blessed with better eyesight than orcs, and a greater ability to see objects in motion. They were able to see the attacks coming their way.

With their strength, which rivaled the ogres, and their smarts, on par with the lizardmen, the bugbears tried to deflect the orc's attack.

It might have worked. But not against Bash.

Even the Human Hero, Ashes the Giant Killer, who had once killed an ogre with his bare hands, could not have parried such blows. Even a dragon, with a hide of thick scales, could not have kept its head on its body in the midst of such an attack.

Bash was an Orc Hero who had slain many a foe and was feared by many more.

The pride of the orcs. There was no one who could survive against him.

The five remaining bugbears were turned into mincemeat in the blink of an eye.

"Oh! Ohhh!"

Boggs's eyes were filled with the horrific sight of his beloved war buddies—which had fought for him for so many years on the battlefield—now reduced to piles of gore.

His hand tightened around the handle of his mace.

Why had he not stepped forward to fight alongside his bugbears?

Why had he not chosen to die with them?

Why had he not taken even one step forward into the fray?

Overcome with guilt and regret, his chest suddenly began to fill up with a yearning for battle, with a thirst for revenge.

But he was afraid of Bash. So afraid.

Boggs had always believed that the fighting spirit, and battle itself, was everything in life. That belief had led him to defy the Orc King, to end up locked in a deadly duel against an Orc Hero. But now, after everything he'd been through, he was too terrified to move.

And he was angry, too...angry with himself.

"Gahhh!!!"

Boggs made a fist and punched himself in the thigh with it.

He stayed as angry as ever, but the fear was gone now, and he found he could move at last.

"*Baaash!*"

Bash was unmoved.

All he thought about was ending the life of the enemy in front of him.

"Boggs!"

As he yelled the other orc's name aloud, flashbacks of his memories of Boggs began to flit through Bash's mind.

Back when Bash had only just joined the war, back when his sword arm was weak and skinny...Bash had seen Boggs one day. Boggs and his bugbears. What an amazing sight it had been, to see them dash across the battlefield in murderous pursuit of the enemy!

And how splendid Boggs had seemed to young Bash, right in the thick of battle, swinging his mace with reckless abandon. How manly, how breathtaking!

Bash had been certain he would never achieve that level of strength.

That's how otherworldly Boggs had seemed.

But Bash had caught up to Boggs. Overtaken him. And now he felt not even one shred of the admiration that had so affected him on the battlefields of his youth.

"Graaagh!"

"Grooo!"

A flash.

Boggs's mace clanged against Bash's greatsword.

Steel scraped against steel. The orc greatsword sent sparks dancing along the surface of the mace as it twisted and bent it into a useless, distorted shape.

The demon-tempered sword continued along the trajectory of Bash's swing, not bending or warping—or indeed suffering any visible damage at all—as it ended its journey embedded deep into Boggs's head.

"Gah..."

Boggs's neck had become a fountain of blood.

"..."

Now headless, Boggs's body fell limply to its knees.

It knelt there for a moment. Then, finally, it slid to the floor with a dull *thud*.

And there lay the beast tamer who had attained the rank of beast master.

The greatest orc to ever tame a pack of wild bugbears was dead.

"Hah..."

Bash let out a sigh and looked around him.

There were no enemies left remaining in the cavern.

All fourteen bugbears had been wiped out in seconds.

There were no surviving bandits left, either. Even if there were, with Boggs gone, there was no way they could continue with their plot.

"Boggs..."

Bash looked down upon Boggs's corpse, thinking on the past.

Every soldier knew Boggs, and his reputation as a beast tamer went far and wide.

Boggs had been doing what he did for so long—for many years before Bash was even born, in fact.

In the midst of what seemed like a hopeless battle, Boggs had spoken to Bash.

"*Bash, you are the pride of orckind. You are the warrior every orc aspires to be like.*"

And Bash had responded:

"*If it hadn't been for you, I would never have survived in battle for so long.*"

Yes, Bash remembered those words and how raw and real those emotions had been.

Boggs was...a truly remarkable warrior.

Bash had been under the impression that Boggs had died in the final battle. He had never dreamed that he would encounter Boggs again out here, as a stateless, rogue orc.

Something must have happened to him. But Bash did not know what. Nor did Bash understand the meaning of Boggs's final words.

Boggs, despicable in Bash's eyes? Not a bit of it. He had respected him.

"Was that the last of them?"

Houston was speaking to Bash now, his face marred by fresh wounds.

It looked like he'd been scratched by a bugbear's filthy claws.

The wounds were red and angry looking. Probably already infected.

"Yeah. I already killed all the bandits farther inside."

"What about Judith and the others?"

"They're farther back. No one has died yet, I don't think."

"I see. That's good news, then, at least. We should carry them back to the town."

Houston was dabbing his wounds with saliva as he spoke.

Bash would be able to handle things alone, Houston had thought. That was why he had prioritized securing the escape route. But Bash had exceeded his expectations.

He had killed fourteen bugbears in rapid succession and even cut down an orc warrior.

Bash truly was an orc worthy of the title of Hero.

...*It's amazing I managed to escape from an orc like that so many times...*

Houston breathed a sigh of relief.

9

†he Proposal

After the battle, Bash and the others went through the cave, gathering up everything that looked like it might have been stolen by the bandits.

Everything matched the itinerary of stolen items Judith had compiled. It seemed there was no mistake. These were the bandits who had directed the bugbears to attack merchant wagons on the highway.

They even found sales records in one room, proving the bandits had been making a profit on the stolen goods.

With this proof in hand, they would even be able to arrest the trading company that had been in cahoots with the bandits.

The case had been completely solved.

Taking the evidence with them, Bash's company left the cave behind.

"It's so bright..."

As they emerged from the dark cover of the forest, the sunlight was dazzling.

Dawn had broken at some point.

Bash narrowed his eyes and surveyed the surrounding area.

The foot soldiers were in a terrible state. Thanks to fairy dust, their health had been stabilized. Still, they needed to lean on one another just to walk.

Judith's heart was heavy as she gazed at the soldiers.

Her beautiful translucent skin and golden hair were both dirty. Her eyes were puffy from crying, with tear streaks visible through the dirt on her cheeks. And yet she seemed to have discovered a new resolve within herself.

To Bash, she was a peerless beauty.

"..."

Judith turned to look at Bash, perhaps sensing his gaze upon her.

But she said nothing. Instead, she pursed her lips and turned away.

Usually, this would have been her cue to snark at him or give him one of her patented evil glares.

But now, she seemed almost embarrassed.

"Boss! Boss!"

As Bash gazed at Judith, Zell appeared by his ear, whispering excitedly to him.

"I have a hunch that you might be able to bed the fair maiden if you strike now!"

"...Really?"

"You saved her from a sticky situation. She saw your strength. I'm not one hundred percent certain, but this is the best chance you're gonna get, I think! And look! Check out her finger!"

Bash looked at Judith's hand with curiosity.

Her ring finger was bare.

"It's your chance, Boss! You gotta take it!"

The word *chance* made Bash's mind start running a mile a minute. Suddenly, he saw himself back in the cave. Judith was there, too, in all her half-naked glory. Translucent skin, exposed breasts, glistening eyes.

Bash began to snort and pant.

He had spent the last twenty-four hours denying himself. After learning about how difficult human women were to win over, Bash had splashed himself in cologne, held his tongue while being harangued, and restrained himself when confronted with the sight of a juicy naked woman...

But now, after so much self-restraint, the lovely female knight he longed for was actually within his grasp.

Bash clenched his fists in excitement.

Then, still gazing at Judith's hand...

"Judith..." Still snorting and panting hard, Bash spoke to her.

"...Wh-what?"

Judith turned around, an annoyed look on her face.

At the sight of Bash, who was panting hard, she gulped a little, her face tensing up. Ignoring this, Bash took hold of Judith's shoulder with one of his meaty hands.

Then he asked her:

"Woman. Do you want to have my babies?"

The standard orc proposal.

"...!"

Judith's eyes widened. Anger flashed across her face.

But the anger only lasted for a moment. Then it cleared.

She stared at Bash for a few seconds and then giggled.

Aha! That's a good sign! thought Bash, his spirits rising. But then Judith spoke.

"You can't scare me, orc. You said, 'The Orc King has strictly forbidden nonconsensual coitus with members of other races,' right?"

Her response was neither a yes nor a no.

Bash's nose was whistling now as he continued to pant.

Confused, Bash decided to consult with his brain.

"Oi, Brain. What does she mean? Was that a yes or a no?"

"Hmm..."

The brain crossed its imaginary arms thoughtfully, weighing the meaning behind Judith's words.

Yes or no? Bash's tiny mind lit up with a mental image. Here was a fairy carrying a placard that read: YES. And here was another fairy holding one that read: NO. The YES and NO fairies suddenly began to fight each other. Fairy dust flew as they punched and kicked. In the end, the brain shook its head solemnly as it judged the winner.

"Hmm, it was close, but I'm afraid you've been rejected."

The brain lifted the fist of the NO fairy high in victory. The fairy blew kisses to the spectating crowd. It was a close call indeed.

"I've been rejected... It's a no..."

"It's a no, Boss."

"So what do I do now?"

"When you've been rejected, the standard response is to give up and move on to the next woman. That's considered proper etiquette. If you continue to push, that's when things move into nonconsensual territory."

"Hmm. I see..."

It didn't look like Bash would be getting what he wanted this time.

"Oh well. It is what it is."

Still, Bash didn't feel too downhearted.

During the war, Bash's side had sometimes lost, no matter how hard he himself had fought.

Not every opportunity led to victory. Sometimes, you had to take the loss on the chin. And you wouldn't last long on the battlefield if you allowed defeat to shake you. You had to pull yourself together and move on to the next battle. That was what it meant to be a warrior.

But...

But Bash was filled with regret.

After all, this had been Bash's first battle on the field of romance.

He wished he could have stuck it out a little longer, even though he knew that stubborn inexperience was the downfall of many a warrior.

"I see. That's a shame. I was quite fond of you."

"Wow, you're handling rejection pretty well for an orc. Out of curiosity, what is it that you see in me? Not only did I openly disrespect you to your face multiple times, but I also disgraced myself by getting captured by the enemy. Then you had to rescue me as I lay there, a blubbering mess. So...why?"

"Well...you're pretty."

"Heh."

Judith laughed. She thought he was making a joke.

"Heh, thanks for the compliment."

Judith smoothed back her matted hair as she spoke.

Bash didn't feel like being polite. His stomach made a funny flipping motion as he watched Judith pull back her golden hair.

Oblivious to Bash's continued lust for her, Judith shrugged.

"Anyway, thank you for saving me. Really. If you hadn't come along, I would have ended up like my older sister..."

"You have a sister?"

"Yeah. She was captured and detained as a war criminal by you orcs. And then she was used as breeding stock and abused until there was nothing left of her..."

"Oh..."

Bash pressed his lips together.

Judith's sister... Bash pictured a beautiful female knight, as lovely as her younger sister.

Bash could well imagine how such a beautiful lady knight would have been treated by the orcs during the war...

At the time, though, no one would have thought anything of it.

The orcs saw all women as targets for capture.

During the peace talks, when the sanctions were being decided, a human female knight had spoken up, cutting down a sole orc warrior. She was known as Lily the Blood Sprayer, and this is what she said:

"*Nonconsensual sex with women of other races... This practice is immensely damaging to the pride of female knights such as myself! If you orcs had any pride in yourselves as a race, you would allow the defeated to choose an honorable death instead! Stop humiliating and debasing us in defeat! Allow us to die on the battlefield with our dignity intact!*"

Her speech went a long way toward enlightening the orcs.

But of course, there were still many orcs who were led by their carnal desires. And many others who saw no point in changing their ways now, after centuries and centuries of such practices. Others were concerned about losing access to breeding opportunities and stood in stubborn opposition.

Not all orcs were like that, though.

"You know, I've always despised orcs because of what happened to my sister... She was so brilliant, so inspiring..."

As Judith spoke, the old dark shadow passed over her features once again.

Her seething hatred was obvious. Her burning desire to murder every last member of orckind...

But then her expression cleared once more.

"But now I've started to change my thinking a little. Now I know that there *are* great men like you among the orc race, that is."

Judith had not let go of her grudge. But it felt a little lighter to bear now.

That's what her expression told Bash.

Bash still didn't really understand the situation. Luckily, Zell did.

The fairy fluttered around Bash's ear, whispering to him.

"Boss...I hate to be the one to tell ya, but this ain't gonna happen."

"Oh, but...she said I'm a great man. Isn't that a good thing?"

"It looks like this woman has the orcs on her no-mate list. Boss, there's certain races you wouldn't want to mate with, too, right?"

Indeed, there were certain races Bash would not like to mate with.

For one, the lizardmen. Bash certainly wouldn't want to sleep with one of their race. Their reptilian features did nothing for him. Besides, you could barely even tell which were the males and which were the females.

Another race on Bash's no-mate list would be the killer bees. Even if he was to mate with one of them, only baby killer bees would be born. Also, the females had a policy of eating the males after becoming pregnant. Bash was hoping his first sexual encounter wouldn't be his last. Killer bees were definitely out.

And there were other races Bash would prefer not to lay with, as well.

It seemed that orcs were one of those races to Judith. If so, then Bash really didn't have a chance.

"Well, she may not be your wife, but she did say you were a great man, and that could lead to other opportunities! Human women like to talk and gossip among themselves, y'know. Even if *she's* not into orcs, she might put in a good word for you with some other women!"

"True!"

Bash pictured a line of women, all just as attractive as Judith.

Ah yes, they were all just Bash's type. It was a shame about Judith, to be sure, but Bash was certain he could find solace with another...

"Oh, but don't go telling her you want her to introduce you to a friend. Women don't like that. They get mad when a guy switches up his attentions too quick, for some reason."

"I see...then what should I say?"

"Hmm... Just say you're looking to meet someone new. If you phrase it that way, it might go well."

Bash nodded thoughtfully.

Zell was so helpful when it came to things like this. If Bash had been alone, he never would have thought of asking.

"Judith. I have a favor to ask."

"Um, you do?"

"I'm looking to meet someone new. A woman. Do you have any idea where I should look?"

Judith frowned thoughtfully at Bash for a second. Then her eyebrows shot up, and she glanced at Houston. He had been listening to their conversation and nodded.

"All right, I think I have an idea."

"Hmm. *You* do?"

"Ha-ha, I'm the Krassel Army general, you know. I do have access to that kind of information."

An army general was equivalent to an orc great warlord.

A great warlord always looked out for his subordinate warriors.

Men who didn't show due care for their juniors would never have become great warlords in the first place, see.

Orcs were a simple race, but they weren't stupid. They knew what it took to be a great commander.

But a great warrior like Bash didn't automatically make for a great commander.

Still, he could appreciate how a general might know much about the female knights under his command. Enough to recommend one or two...

"You should journey to the Shiwanashi Forest, in elf country. If you do that, I'm certain you'll have the encounter you seek."

"The elves, eh...?"

That wasn't quite the introduction Bash had been expecting.

He had been sure Houston was going to introduce him to another sexy female human knight.

But an elf would do nicely. They weren't as fertile as humans, but they were fully capable of conceiving from sex with orcs. And any children they bore Bash would be blessed with magical power.

Plus, they were long-lived and very durable, and some of them were extreme beauties. As a result, they were very sought-after among the orc race.

Some orcs didn't care for them, though. For many orcs, the typical elf was far too skinny.

But Bash wasn't opposed to elves at all. In fact, elves were considered something of a rarity at the time, since there were few to be found in orc country. If Bash returned home with an elf bride, his standing as an Orc Hero would only be boosted.

"An elf... Not bad. Not bad at all, Boss!"

"Right! Well, we'd better head there right away."

Bash was satisfied. He turned to leave. Seeing this, Houston frowned in confusion.

"Hmm? Where are you going?"

"To Shiwanashi Forest."

Indeed, Shiwanashi Forest wasn't far, but it was in the opposite direction of the Fortified City of Krassel.

There was no need for Bash to return to the town.

"Well, don't you want to stay the night in Krassel? You'd be very welcome."

"I don't have time."

Bash wanted to be rid of his virginity as soon as possible.

If Shiwanashi Forest was where he could make that happen, then he didn't want to waste another second.

"But I thought we could all have drinks together at the tavern tonight to celebrate our success..."

Houston wanted to keep Bash around a little longer, but he knew better than to push. Instead, he decided to drop it and chuckled.

"All right, then. I understand. We won't detain you."

The foot soldiers hadn't been following the conversation and turned after the orc in confusion upon realizing he was leaving.

But neither Houston nor Judith said anything.

They simply watched Bash go. But then Judith took a step forward.

"Mr. Bash..."

Bash came to a stop. His heart filled with a sudden wild hope.

"May the fortunes of war be in your favor."

The hope faded as quickly as it had come.

But Bash looked back over his shoulder at Judith and nodded firmly.

Then he turned again and began walking in the direction of the Shiwanashi Forest.

"We didn't really catch all the details, but why did that orc come to Krassel, again?"

When they had almost reached the town gates, one of the soldiers posed this question.

"Hmm? Isn't it obvious?"

"Sir, if you wouldn't mind explaining it..."

Houston thought it over for a second, his gaze sliding to Judith.

You know, don't you? Enlighten them. That's what his look said.

Judith sighed and yet launched into an explanation anyway.

"After the war, the Orc King outlawed fighting and opted for peace. You know that much, right?"

"Yes, of course. General Houston was at the signing ceremony for the peace treaty, as I recall."

"Right. Well, even among the orcs who were at the signing, there were those who were opposed to the new terms."

"You mean they didn't want peace with the humans?"

"Exactly. For orcs, fighting comes as naturally as breathing. From the moment they're born, they dream of going to war. Peace was a ludicrous concept to them. They wanted to continue fighting and creating havoc. There were a lot of orcs who held that view."

The soldier swallowed hard.

"Those who were opposed ended up leaving orc country and scattering themselves across the world. Then they caused chaos in all sorts of other countries. Like what happened in our country, in the forest."

Judith knew a lot about orc culture and history. She'd learned from Houston.

Moreover, she'd spent a year shadowing him and learning his method for hunting down the rogue orcs.

She knew what they were like.

Half of them were despicable, the dregs of society, and not particularly skilled warriors, either. Nor could they manage to obey the orders of the Orc King.

But there was another type of rogue orc out there.

The best of the warrior class. The ones who had survived countless battles and slain hundreds of enemies. They were both strong and cunning. They knew how to survive.

"The incident this time—that was definitely caused by an orc. But what does that have to do with the journey Mr. Bash said he was on?"

"You still don't know, even after everything you've just heard?"

Judith shrugged, rolling her eyes.

"Mr. Bash is out in the world, seeking out these shameful rogue orcs, and exterminating them one by one."

Judith thought she had figured out Bash's mission. Bash was a true soldier, able to put aside his own desires and show loyalty to his commanding lord. That's why he kept bringing up the Orc King so many times. And the thing the Orc King and the Hero Bash were both trying to protect was...

"So he's out there trying to restore the pride of the orc race."

Orcs were wild and uncouth. Most other races had this sort of negative impression of them.

Of course, this impression wasn't exactly wrong.

At the same time, though, the orcs were proud of their race.

And they were fully prepared to reap what they had sown in the war.

In order to restore the reputation of the orcs, they had dispatched their finest Hero, Bash, on a divine mission. *How could it be anything else?* thought Judith.

"This incident has changed my impression of the orc race, just a little."

Judith had despised orcs.

It was orcs who had violated her sister, who had shown themselves incapable of respect toward other races, and particularly their women.

They saw women as little more than breeding stock. There was no way Judith could ever look upon their kind with fondness.

But even among that race she hated so much, there was at least one whom she found worthy of her respect.

As a knight, there was at least one orc who had inspired her.

This realization felt somehow incredibly significant to Judith.

Her mind had been opened to new possibilities.

"But, General Houston, you knew what was going on from the start, didn't you? You knew right away why Mr. Bash came to Krassel."

"Hmm... Well."

Houston chuckled airily. Actually, when he had first realized Bash was in town, he had almost wet his pants. But it was also obvious straight away that Bash was there on some sort of mission. After so many years spent studying orc culture and behaviors, he'd figured that out right away. Yes, dedicating himself to the study of the orcs had been his greatest tool for self-preservation.

And armed with that knowledge, Houston had been able to comport himself around the orc without causing any offense. Even better, he'd been able to help him on his mission.

Houston felt proud of himself for that.

"We should all strive to be like that orc if we have any pride in ourselves as knights."

"You're right. I, personally, intend to dedicate myself to my work in the hopes of being more like Mr. Bash."

Judith sighed deeply, thinking back over recent events, her resolve firm and her heart full.

She would never forget meeting Bash.

She would never forget how he had acted with honor and pride.

She would become a great warrior, too, just like Bash...

"But first, you're all in for some serious pay cuts and a period of deep self-reflection as penance for your mutinous actions in that cave. But you'll keep your titles in honor of the great Orc Hero Bash!"

"Y-yes, sir!"

"Yessir! *Yessir!*"

Houston and Judith exchanged smiles.

Both were grateful to the fates for allowing them to cross paths with someone like Bash. In high spirits, the company set off to return to their home, the Fortified City of Krassel.

EPİLOGUE

Bash was making his way through the forest.

His destination: the Shiwanashi Forest in elf country.

The forest was thick and overgrown, but Bash picked his way through, sure-footed as ever.

Relying on the fairy to navigate, Bash simply placed one foot in front of the other in pursuit of his destination.

"Shiwanashi Forest is pretty close! We'll be there in no time."

"Right!"

Bash and Zell, reunited.

Both had made names for themselves in the war. As a pair, they went together well.

During the war, they had survived countless battles by working together. While there had been some crushing defeats, they had always made it through.

So even though Bash's first attempt at wife hunting had ended in failure, they were confident the second time would go better. But even if they failed again, there would be another chance after that.

After all, things had always been that way.

Their destination, the Shiwanashi Forest.

Both believed Bash would find a bride there, and then their journey could come to an end.

They still had no idea.

No idea how long a journey this would really turn out to be.

Around the same time...

An elf made an appearance at a human party.

A glamorous party for the human aristocracy.

Everywhere you looked, gorgeously dressed ladies and gentlemen were engaged in pleasant conversation.

A man and a woman were laughing together. During the war, the man had barely ever cracked a smile. The woman had bared her teeth and bellowed war cries on the battlefield. Now they chuckled loudly.

In the midst of the party, a certain elf was deep in conversation with the son of a nobleman.

They were discussing the future of the human race.

"Hmm. I believe that this era will place a higher value than ever before on commerce and education, as well as the arts."

"I see... Well, I'd like to establish schools all over the human country, but all we have are ex-soldiers and knights. We lack cultured individuals who would make for good teachers..."

"And those who are cultured are already in pursuit of their own career interests."

"Right. Actually, I'm working to consult with them on creating materials, some sort of handbook to be used in training up a new generation of teachers. I was hoping we might be able to get the elf input on that."

"A primer for educators! Actually, we elves were thinking of something similar. It is so like humans to seek to preserve knowledge in tangible form, isn't it? Ah, but I meant no offense! How about meeting up this evening to discuss the future of education in further detail?"

"Ha-ha-ha. I appreciate your proposal, but won't people get the wrong idea if a man and a woman meet after hours, alone?"

"What?! I mean... Heh... Surely, Lord Merz, the Battering Ram, isn't concerned about idle gossip?"

"Oh, I am concerned."

"You... You are?"

"Don't test me, please. We're not all out to make enemies of every elf alive, you know."

"Ah, of course, of course! Ha-ha, yes, yes, of course! Ha-ha!"

The elf laughed as well. But her laugh was somewhat sardonic, not at all like the innocent laughter of the guests around her.

She still had no idea.

No idea that another would soon come to share her objective. A Hero of the orc race.

A young female dwarf was sharpening a sword in a workshop somewhere.

The workshop was filled with the scraping sound of the sword being worked upon.

After working on the sword for a few moments more, she plunged it carefully into the bucket she had beside her. As the sword sank into the red water that filled the bucket, something like black dust rose to the water's surface.

She withdrew the blade from the water and admired it.

"...Good!"

"What's good?"

"...!"

The girl whirled around to see another female dwarf standing there.

"I thought I told you never to come into my workshop uninvited."

"It's your fault. You should have locked the door. What are you working on? What's with that bright-red water? Did you put paint in it or something?"

"My work is secret. I can't have people stealing my techniques."

"Pah! You assume your techniques are even worth stealing. If you've got the time to mess about with silly things like that, then you could spend a few minutes more sharpening your creations properly!"

"Tch! You're always acting like such a supercilious snob! Is that really what you came in here to say?"

The intruder sighed as the young dwarf's rage bubbled over.

"I'd rather not have to say it at all. But who could stay silent, seeing such shoddy work?"

"How dare you mock me! Don't expect any sympathy when I see you crying at the next God of War Festival!"

"Ha, the festival? That's way beyond your pathetic abilities!"

With that final snooty remark, the other woman stormed out of the workshop.

The young girl left behind gnashed her teeth for a moment, gazing at her sword.

She still had no idea.

No idea that one day, that very same sword of hers would be wielded by a Hero of the orc race.

The beastkin princess was in her chambers, gazing listlessly out the window.

Below her window, she could see the new town.

After the war, the town had been built within a mere three-year timespan. Everything was still so new, but the old customs remained. It was a mishmash of a town, to be sure, but it was lively and exciting.

The beastkin royal family was keen to make the town prosper.

The princess didn't know much about it all, but this town was built on holy land that had once been stolen away from the beastkin.

Until the Beastkin Champion Rett had taken it back.

Every resident of the town felt a great sense of pride toward him.

In the battle to take down the Demon Lord Geddigs, Rett had died a hero. They had each dealt a killing blow simultaneously.

Rett was the greatest legend in all of beastkin history, the pride of their race...

"If they really respected Rett as much as they claim, then why must they spew these lies?"

The truth was different.

Oh, the part about Rett being a hero was all true, of course.

But the facts behind the history differed in one key area. In order to preserve the good name of the hero and protect the pride of the beastkin race, they were all required to lie about that.

It did not sit well with the princess.

"The truth must be dug up and exposed."

The princess stared out the window, her expression twisted with hate. But it was not the town she was seeing in her mind's eye. She was focused inside, ruminating on the dark sentiments of her soul.

"I must have revenge. As tribute to Uncle Rett."

She still had no idea.

No idea that the truth she clung to was actually false.

Nor did she ever dream that all would come to light with the help of an Orc Hero.

A girl watched her twin brother.

He was doggedly swinging his sword.

She had always watched him practice, but it was plain to see that he had no skill with the sword. That's not to say he didn't have the potential. But self-study would not lead him to greatness; that much was clear.

"Hyah! Hyah!"

"Have some water, Brother."

"Thanks."

The boy took the canteen and gulped down the contents. Then he resumed swinging his sword.

The twins had a foe they needed to defeat. An enemy of their father and mother both. A powerful enemy.

That was why the boy was practicing.

His mind was singularly focused on striking down their enemy with his blade of vengeance.

"...Brother, the sun is setting."

"Just a little longer."

"...I'm heading back first."

The boy continued to swing the sword, not answering.

The girl sighed a little, watching him.

She had given up. Their enemy was far too powerful to be felled by someone like her brother, even if he practiced the sword for months or even years straight.

Of course, she wanted revenge for her parents as well. But she had managed to repress such emotions. Now all she feared was losing her brother, her only remaining blood.

Never was she able to ask him to give up, however.

"If only someone out there would kill them so we don't have to..."

She still had no idea.

No idea that their quest for revenge would be brought to an end by an Orc Hero.

A succubus was lying down in a wasteland beneath a sky full of stars.

Below, the lights of a town were twinkling. But she wasn't looking at the town. She was simply gazing at the sky.

She was thinking of long ago. Of those who had fought so many times during the war.

It was better back then. You didn't have to think. You just fought to the point of exhaustion and then slept like a log. But not too deeply, of course. And then you would be jolted awake by reports of impending enemy attacks.

She had always been tired. But at the same time, fulfilled.

Now, though, I have entirely too much time to think.

She thought about the events that led her to having to sleep outdoors like this.

She had been driven out of the town, denied lodgings for no other reason than because she was a succubus.

"Peace sucks."

She pictured the face of the mayor, the faces of the townspeople, who could barely hide their looks of disgust the moment they spotted a succubus in their midst.

Their words had been all scorn and mockery.

The war was over. The world was at peace.

That was what people said. But there was no peace for the succubi. Peace was a privilege that only certain races got to enjoy.

"They all deserve to die."

The succubus gazed up at the stars.

At that very moment, in a desert somewhere, a certain orc was gazing up at the stars as well.

She still had no idea.

No idea that real peace would soon be brought to the world by an Orc Hero.

Dragon had a friend, Bones. They were always together. They were together even now.

Bones was a peculiar dragon.

Bones was very interested in people and would often go down to the villages and scare them.

Dragon did not know why Bones did this. People were tiny, with barely enough meat for a decent snack. It was better to leave them alone.

But Bones was very, very interested in people. Eventually, Bones even mated with one and sired an egg.

In the past, such dragons had existed, or so went the tales. But it seemed impossible to understand.

Still, Dragon didn't mind odd folks.

And Bones's tales of the people's funny doings were amusing to listen to.

Even if the stories themselves weren't very interesting, Dragon liked to see Bones talking with so much enthusiasm.

Then one day, Bones died.

A puny person had come by and persuaded Bones to follow them somewhere.

After that, Bones came back as...well...bones.

Bones had fought with the people soldiers in the war and died.

Bones's body was collected by the ones who had slain him. Apparently, people found dragon bodies very valuable.

Bones came back to Dragon. But the puny people who had taken Bones away brought back only the skull of Bones.

The people apologized to Dragon.

Dragon felt sadness for the first time in her life. Never before had she experienced the passing of one of her own. She did not fully understand. But seeing how deeply the little people apologized to Dragon, Dragon eventually realized that something had happened to Bones that could never be undone.

Dragon spent a full year in sadness. Every now and then, to soothe her pain, she would fly to the towns and gobble up some of the little people. Why had Bones gotten involved in their insignificant people war? It did not make sense to Dragon.

Then, all of a sudden, Dragon began to experience something she had never felt before.

Curiosity.

Dragon started to get curious about people. How had these tiny, weak beings, who ran screaming from Dragon, managed to kill Bones?

She still had no idea.

No idea that the one who had slain Bones was an Orc Hero.

Bonus Story
Judith After Bash

Around three days had passed since Judith's encounter with Bash.

That day, Judith was ordered to patrol the highway with the foot soldiers under her command.

The issue of the highway ambushes had been solved, but they were being sent out just to make sure there were no new developments on the road. She had been ordered to check that there were no survivors from the cave bandit group. If all looked well, they were to clean up the road while they were out there.

Judith's group consisted of herself and just a few men, incidentally the same ones who had been involved in solving the bandit case with her.

In other words, this task was a punishment for them all.

Houston was pragmatic. He knew that allowing their mutiny to go unpunished would set a bad precedent to the others. Also, he thought a self-imposed period of quiet reflection would be nothing but a waste of valuable workforce.

So his solution to both of those issues was to send them out on this pointless busywork.

"A few days of hard work on the roads without a break—that'll do as punishment for the likes of you lot."

Houston's words had surprised them all.

Still, knowing they'd gotten off lightly, Judith and the men set out onto the road, accepting the orders they had been given.

They all assumed the task would proceed without incident.

However, that was not how it would unfold. Once Judith and company reached the highway, a single orc came creeping out of the forest.

He was a regular green orc, a battle-ax in one hand and a large club strapped to his back.

If it came to a fight, perhaps he meant to dual wield its weapons.

"It's an orc. Hey, you there. What are you doing here?"

If this had happened back before she met Bash, Judith would have already given the order to attack. But now that she'd made Bash's acquaintance, she was willing to shrug and walk right past a random orc who happened to appear in the forest.

Only, she was technically on a mission. She was duty-bound to question whatever suspicious individuals she saw in the forest that day.

"Who says I have ta tell the likes of you?"

"I'm Judith, a knight from Krassel. We're patrolling the highway at this time."

"Heh! That voice, that name...a female knight, are ye?"

The orc gave her a lecherous grin.

It was the kind of grin that told her he was thinking about throwing her to the ground and violating her on the spot.

But Judith looked closer. He had strong arms, yes, but unlike Bash, he had a protruding potbelly. And unlike Bash, he didn't really have any kind of dignified air about him at all.

"A rogue orc, huh?"

"Heh, what's it to ya?"

"Nothing, really. Just wondering why you rogue orcs are wandering around out here, why you couldn't uphold the word of your Orc King."

"Pah! Ain't it obvious? The orcs are done for. We've lost our pride. Everyone's just living like cattle, the same day over an' over again! You humans call us orcs pigs, right? Well, maybe yer right! We've lost the will ta even get mad!"

"So that's why you've left your country?"

"Damn right! I'm gonna travel the world an' show the people all about the great orc race! I'll start with you, Lady Knight! I'm gonna squirt me seed up in ya an' make ya birth me babies!"

Judith grimaced in disgust.

Then she thought about the orc she had met only three days prior. His calm expression and his careful way of speaking.

"Wow, there really is a huge difference between the Orc Hero and one of you rogues, isn't there?"

"A Hero? What does a human wench like you know of Bash?"

"I met him just the other day, actually."

"...What?"

"He's the one who's actually out here repairing the reputation of the orcs. With honor and dignity, too, not despair and self-abandonment like you pathetic rogues."

"Bash is...repairin' the reputation of the orcs?"

"Yep."

Then Judith told the rogue orc all about what had happened a few days ago.

About how Bash had been a perfect gentleman. About how he had remained gracious despite her own human rudeness and disrespect. About how Bash had come to her rescue when she had acted like a fool. She told him all of it.

She also told him about her own hunch, that Bash had embarked upon his journey out of a sense of loyalty to his race.

"I can't believe a manly orc like Bash would keep it in his pants with a female knight like you right in front of 'im!"

"That's because Mr. Bash isn't a rogue like you. He abides by the rules of the Orc King. Even if that means denying his own drive. As a result, even a fool such as I now understands the true pride of the orcs!"

"I was wonderin' where Bash went off to; ain't seen 'im for days..."

"He's sacrificed his own desires for the good of his race. Why don't you try to learn from his example?"

As Judith spoke, she unsheathed her sword.

Despite their dialogue, Judith knew better than to expect anything much of a rogue orc. He probably saw her as nothing but a shrill, overly talkative woman trying to buy time before being roughly taken and impregnated.

It had always gone like that.

Judith had only had dealings with rogue orcs a few times, yes, but each time, it had ended in a fight to the death.

"..."

"Hmm?"

The rogue orc was backing down.

Lowering the battle-ax, it retreated several steps, as if the will to fight had left it.

"What are you doing? Where are you going?"

"Ain't it obvious? I'm goin' home."

"That's...unusual. Every rogue orc I've come across before now has come flying at me in a rage the second I confront them..."

"Yeah, it don't sit well with me to be turnin' me back an' retreatin' from a stuck-up human wench like you. But if Bash is out there tryin' ta repair the reputation of the orc race, I can't very well be doin' things ta mess that up. But if ya really wanna throw down with me, I won't deny ya the chance. I'm an orc, after all, and I've got me pride..."

"No, no, if you plan to return home, then I won't stop you."

The orc snorted a laugh and walked away.

Judith watched him go, feeling slightly deflated.

She had been so convinced that rogue orcs were beyond reasoning with. Wasn't that why she had always been so heavy-handed with them? Why Houston had always instantly issued the order to kill?

The rogue orc had been as stubborn and unpleasant as all the rest.

But it was strange.

At the mere mention of Bash's name, the rogue orc seemed to return to some semblance of his warrior past and had retreated honorably.

Orc Hero. The title had sounded impressive enough to Judith, but it clearly carried far more weight back in Bash's homeland. The title of Hero itself seemed to come with a great deal of trust and respect, even reverence.

"If Bash's name can have that kind of sobering effect on even a foul rogue orc like that...then it's clear we met with a far more important person than we ever could have imagined..."

The soldiers were muttering things like that among themselves.

Judith shared their sentiments. The Orc Hero Bash... Compared to the rogue orc she'd just seen...no, compared to all the *humans* she'd met in her life so far, no one seemed more worthy of the Hero title than he.

"That's why Houston treated Bash with such reverence..."

"Next time you see Bash, are you gonna treat him with that kind of reverence, too, Judith?"

"Maybe next time he asks you to have his babies, you won't turn him down, eh?"

Judith hated orcs. The mere sight of one made her skin crawl.

"All jokes aside, let's hurry and check that bandit hideout one more time. Houston is going to work us hard again tomorrow, too. We're going to have to work hard enough to make up for disrespecting Mr. Bash before Houston's satisfied."

"You're the one who disrespected Mr. Bash, Judith. We just followed you."

"Oh, shut up and get moving."

Judith smiled wryly to herself. Yes, she still hated the orcs. With one very special exception.

AFTERWORD

Hello, it's nice to meet you. Or if you've read one of my works before, then hello again. I'm Rifujin na Magonote.

I'd like to take this opportunity to express my gratitude to you all for picking up this copy of *Orc Eroica*.

Thank you all very much.

I'd like to be able to write something cool like, "I dedicate this book to...," but I unfortunately don't have many friends, and I'm all about that bachelor life, so I don't have anyone to dedicate this book to. Maybe someday...

Incidentally, this is my first time writing an afterword, and I didn't even know what to write at first.

So I decided to ask Twitter. I was told I should write about what inspired me to tell this story, about the circumstances that led to it. So I'll do just that.

When it comes to the inspiration behind this book, I can't explain that without telling you about how I first met Editor U.

I actually can't remember very well how we first met. I might have to make up a few details to fill the gaps, so please bear with me.

It was the year 199X. The earth was enveloped in the fires of a nuclear holocaust. A guy with a Mohican haircut was riding his motorbike around and around my neighborhood. Yes, that part is all true.

Always the shut-in, I was barricaded in my house as usual, opening up my author page on the Let's Become a Novelist website. I was hoping I could finish reading all the comments on *Mushoku Tensei: Jobless Reincarnation* before the Mohican managed to break his way in.

Just then, a message popped up in red text. It said that I should respond if I was interested in working together with the sender.

At the time, I had finished *Mushoku Tensei* and hadn't even thought about starting on my next project yet.

I didn't really want to work with them, nor was I particularly interested, but I sent a response anyway.

Then guess what they said? They said I should come to Nagoya at once, and they'd take me to dinner on the Editorial Department's dime.

I jumped at the chance. I had been barricaded inside for three days already, and supplies were running low.

I made arrangements to meet Editor U, the sender of the messages, and ran out of the house.

That's when I realized I'd been tricked.

The Mohican was lying in wait for me outside, holding a bat with a nail in it...

So, that's how I first met Editor U.

After that, we infiltrated Southern Cross together, climbed the Cross Mausoleum together, attacked the village to get to the well together, blew up the village, yelling "Uwaraba!" together, and read the erotic light novel *Dotei Orc no Boken Tan (The Virgin Orc's Adventure Story)* together. Somehow, this turned into me starting to write *Orc Eroica*, but I'll save the details for another time...

Well, now that I've hit my minimum word count, I'll get serious. I have a feeling people are only going to get mad at me if I carry on this way.

This title, *Orc Eroica*, is the story of an Orc Hero who sets out to get rid of his virginity and finds himself saving all kinds of different people, and saving whole countries and that sort of thing, in the meantime.

Maybe he doesn't go through a great deal of character growth in the story, but I hope readers can have a few chuckles along the way and feel a little inspired by his journey. That's the kind of story I was aiming for.

Everyone, I really hope you'll come along with me on this journey.

Thank you very much for being here.

Okay, let's try this again.

To all in the Editorial Department, to Asanagi for the wonderful and suggestive artwork, to Editor K for putting up with me being distracted by *Mushoku Tensei* stuff and making their job a lot harder, to everyone else who was involved in the publishing of this book...

And, of course, to everyone who enjoyed reading this book and who sent me encouragement along the way, thank you very much.

Rifujin na Magonote

Second Wife Candidate:
Thunder Sonia

Book Two:
Elf Country

In the next volume...

Searching for his next wife candidate, Bash arrives in elf country and makes a startling discovery.

"I've made a startling discovery! It's crazy! Really, really crazy!"

"What is it?"

"You'll never believe it! It's unbelievable! Right now, in elf country..."

"...There's been a massive boom in cross-racial marriages!!!"

Is this the perfect opportunity for our Orc Hero to snag himself a bride?!

Already hugely popular with online fans, the character Thunder Sonia finally makes her debut!

COMING SOON

THE SHIWANASHI FOREST SAGA

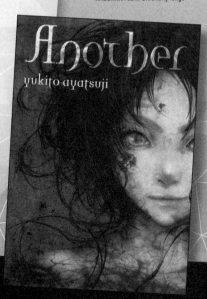